Gregory Maguire is a bestselling author who has earned rave reviews and a dedicated following for *Wicked*, the first novel in the *Wicked Years* quartet (which also included *Son of a Witch*, *A Lion Among Men* and *Out of Oz*), that was made into an award-winning musical. Maguire has lectured on art, literature and culture at home and abroad. He lives with his family near Boston, USA.

Praise for AFTER ALICE

'Maguire conjures up a vision of Victorian England that ranges across its stuffiness, its snobbery and its cruelties' *SFX*

'Thoughtful and disconcertingly memorable . . . This is a feast for the mind, and readers will ruminate on it long after turning the last page' *Publishers Weekly*

'A brilliant and nicely off-kilter reading of the children's classic, retrofitted for grown-ups – and a lot of fun' *Kirkus Reviews*

Acclaim for GREGORY MAGUIRE

'. . . a credible Oz for grown-ups, with religion, politics, racial tensions, an economy, mythology, humour and sex . . . As moving and tragic as it is refreshing and scurrilous . . . outstanding' *Independent*

'A vision that fantasy writers will find hard to resist' *Publishers Weekly*

'Highly absorbing . . . Maguire's precise, slightly archaic language . . . sweeps the readers through this mysterious and fascinating story' *Booklist*

By Gregory Maguire and available from Headline

Confessions of an Ugly Stepsister
Mirror Mirror
Lost
The Next Queen of Heaven
After Alice

Novels in the Wicked Years
Wicked
Son of a Witch
A Lion Among Men
Out of Oz

AFTER ALICE

GREGORY MAGUIRE

headline

Published in the United States in 2015 by
WILLIAM MORROW
An imprint of HarperCollins Publishers

First published in Great Britain in 2015 by
HEADLINE PUBLISHING GROUP

First published in Great Britain in paperback in 2016 by
HEADLINE PUBLISHING GROUP

1

Cataloguing in Publication Data is available from the British Library

ISBN 978 1 4722 3046 1

Typeset in Columbus MT by Palimpsest Book Production Ltd, Falkirk, Stirlingshire

Printed and bound in Great Britain by Clays Ltd, St Ives plc

HEADLINE PUBLISHING GROUP
An Hachette UK Company
Carmelite House
50 Victoria Embankment
London, EC4Y 0DZ

www.headline.co.uk
www.hachette.co.uk

For Natacha Liuzzi

A lice took up the fan and gloves, and, as the hall was very hot, she kept fanning herself all the time she went on talking: 'Dear, dear! How queer everything is to-day! And yesterday things went on just as usual. I wonder if I've been changed in the night? Let me think: *was* I the same when I got up this morning? I almost think I can remember feeling a little different. But if I'm not the same, the next question is "Who in the world am I?" Ah, *that's* the great puzzle!' And she began thinking over all the children she knew that were of the same age as herself, to see if she could have been changed for any of them.

'I'm sure I'm not Ada,' she said, 'for her hair goes in such long ringlets, and mine doesn't go in ringlets at all; and I'm sure I can't be Mabel, for I know all sorts of things, and she, oh! she knows such a very little! Besides, *she's* she, and *I'm* I, and oh dear, how puzzling it all is!'

– LEWIS CARROLL,
ALICE'S ADVENTURES IN WONDERLAND

I appreciate the kind advice of early readers: Ann Fitch, Betty Levin, Andy Newman, Jill Paton Walsh, and of course my editor, Cassie Jones. Any errors of fact, tone, or interpretation are my own. The portion of *The History of the Fairchild Family,* quoted nearly verbatim here in chapter 6, is by Martha Mary Butt Sherwood; the text comes from the chapter called 'The Story on the Sixth Commandment', a section often deleted in later editions of that popular children's novel. The scrap of Victorian poetry recited in chapter 28 is from a chapter header in *Middlemarch;* I'm unable to identify poem or author.

PART THE FIRST

The meteorological records for these parts assure us that July 4, 1862, was 'cool and rather wet': but on that day Lewis Carroll first told the tale of *Alice in Wonderland* to four people in a Thames gig, rowing upstream for a picnic tea, and to the ends of their lives all four remembered the afternoon as a dream of cloudless English sunshine.

– JAMES/JAN MORRIS, *OXFORD*, PAGE 18

CHAPTER 1

Were there a god in charge of story – I mean one cut to Old Testament specifics, some hybrid of Zeus and Father Christmas – such a creature, such a deity, might be looking down upon a day opening in Oxford, England, a bit past the half-way mark of the nineteenth century.

This part of Oxfordshire being threaded with waterways, such a god might have to make a sweep of His mighty hand to clear off the mists of dawn.

Now, to the human renewing the pact with dailiness, Oxford at matins can seem to congeal through the fogs. A process of accretion through light, the lateral sedimentation of reality. A world emerging, daily, out of nothing, a world that we trust to resemble what we've seen previously. We should know better.

To a deity lolling overhead on bolsters of zephyr, however, the city rises as if out of some underground sea, like Debussy's *La cathédrale engloutie,* that fantasia about the submerged Breton cathedral rising once every hundred years off the island of Ys. (Yes, Debussy is early twentieth century, but time means nothing to Himself.) Spires and domes like so much barnacled spindrift poke through first. Gradually, as the sun coaxes the damp away, the coving spaces emerge. From above, not only the lanes and high street, but also the hidden places wink into being. Nooks and wells of secret green in college quadrangles scarcely imagined by the farrier on his way to the stable, the fishmonger to his stall.

An underworld, all exposed by light.

Even Jehovah, presuming Jehovah, must find the finicky architecture of his Oxford too attractive to notice the humbler margins of the district. At least at first. Gods have to wake up, too. But this story starts on the northeast side of town. People are rousing in an old rectory, here, and an even older farmhouse, over there. Night-time is being brushed aside like so much cobweb. The day is wound up and begins even before the last haunted dreams, the last of the fog, those spectral and evanescent residues, have faded away.

CHAPTER 2

'A lice is missing.'

A sigh, a clink of porcelain on porcelain. 'Again?'

CHAPTER 3

Depending upon the hour, a governess in a troubled household is either a ministering angel or an ambulatory munitions device. Behold Miss Armstrong, foraying in the upstairs corridor towards her employer.

'Reverend Boyce? It's about Ada. The child is underfoot and making of herself a nuisance. Underfoot and underhanded; I believe she pesters the poor creature when our backs are turned. Ada must be got outdoors for some healthful exercise. I won't say *mischief,* I just won't. But her absence would allow the household some calm. I assume you've tried Dalby's Carminative? Or Mrs Winslow's Soothing Syrup? Opium has such a tender effect.'

Miss Armstrong hovered in the doorway to the nursery where Ada's brother was not, just now, sleeping. Not any more. The governess stood to let the night nurse pass. The infant castoff reeked with a vegetable accent as the nurse hurried by. She swung the tin pail at the end of her extended arm.

The Vicar mumbled something. It was hard to be sure just what he meant. He specialized in tones of such subtlety that one could hear in it whatever one chose. 'Ada . . .' He backed against the distempered wall, allowing his voice to drift into a nearly musical ellipsis. Miss Armstrong paused, an ear uplifted, waiting for an epiphany. He might have meant anything by it. He faded without clarifying.

Miss Armstrong took his vatic murmur as agreement that an

outing for Ada would do the household good. So the governess cornered Ada on the stair landing, crowding her into the aspidistra. A pot of Mama's best rough-cut would be dislodged from the larder so the child might deliver it somewhere. Perhaps to the benighted family at the Croft? As a mercy. 'We shall go together along the river if you take care not to stumble into the brink and drown,' suggested Miss Armstrong. The river was slow here, our old Cherwell, but kitted out with treacherous tree roots and crumbling banks, and just enough depth to scare one towards salvation. 'Go and say farewell to your mother whilst I collect the marmalade.'

Since members of the household staff argued over competing therapies with which to treat the pink smudge of infant, Mama had repaired to the sewing room. Keeping out of the fray. On this bright morning, the room was still dusky, the curtains not yet drawn back. 'Stay quite a long time if you like. If they'll have you,' said Mama. 'Your brother sorely needs some quiet.'

'It's not my fault if Father likes me to practise my hymns,' said Ada.

'You may practise them all you like in the cow pasture.'

Ada, not a deeply imaginative child, believed the cows were resistant to conversion. She didn't reply.

'If they press you to take tea, accept.'

Ada thought it unlikely that the cows would propose afternoon tea. She blinked, noncommittal. Mama sighed and continued. '*Ada*. Attend. Make yourself a comfort to the Clowds. Endeavour to help in all matters. Play with Alice, perhaps.'

'Alice is a flaming eejit.' Ada gave the word a spin such as Cook, from County Mayo, was wont to do. Mama might have boxed Ada's ears for impertinence: cruelty as well as a mocking Irishry of tone. But her mother knew Ada's outburst was misplaced emotion. An infant in peril affected everyone in the house. And during ordinary hours, Ada was known to be fond of Alice, who was Ada's best friend and her only one. So Mama waggled her fingers in the air, *Go, go,* and settled her crown of hair, the colour of browning roses, upon the bolster of the davenport. A miasma of lavender toilet water couldn't mask the hint of Madeira wafting from the open decanter though it was not yet eleven in the morning. Mrs Boyce lay squalid in self-forgiveness.

Ada considered refusing to be dismissed. But she was a good girl. On the way out, she slammed the sewing room door only a little.

In the front passage, Miss Armstrong handed the marmalade to Ada. 'Off and away with the fairies once again,' said the governess, 'for our sins,' and then she turned to plunge down a few steps towards the kitchen, to hector Cook into warming some milk. His Lordship the Infant Tyrant must be cozened. No alcoholic pap for *him.*

But *off and away with the fairies?* Ada was prosaic. She didn't know to whom the governess referred. The Tiny Interruption, who preferred screaming rather than observing the newborn's usual practice of sleeping round the clock? Or perhaps Ada herself, hulked upon the Indian-red Kidderminster by the front door, staring at her face in the looking-glass? The face appearing between ringlets, Ada thought, *might* be considered innocent and blameless as a fairy. Though ugly. A bad fairy, perhaps. A rotten packet of fairy. She opened the front door without permission, the quicker to get away from the sight of herself standing all clumpedy-clump and iron-spined in the front hall.

'Off and away with the fairies . . .' Without much remorse, Ada decided to behave as if she'd been sent packing, and left.

Cook, hearing the front door bang, gave Miss Armstrong a piece of her mind. 'Sure and ye've dispatched that lummoxing gallootress to foul mischief by tramps and peddlers or to a watery grave, Jaysus mercy are ye out of yer mind like the rest of us?' She threw a marrow at the governess. Miss Armstrong didn't

care to take bosh from someone beneath her. Yet Cook had a
point. Miss Armstrong, whose skills as a governess were heightened by a permanent agitation of the nerves, rushed to hunt for
her gloves so she could pursue Ada with adequate decorum.

The river seen between full-headed trees caught snips of
sunlight and flashed brazen glints. Willows twitched in the wind.
Ada noticed and didn't notice. She had never before ventured
outside without a chaperone. All too soon Miss Armstrong would
ambush her, so through the gate of the Vicarage of Saint Dunstan's
Ada torqued and bumbled. A rare treat, to snatch a few moments
alone. From an upstairs window, her brother's sedition: serrated
syllables, all caw and no coo.

Even here, on the city's northeast edge, where the river and
sky could aspire to eternal bucholia, clouds of stone dust dulled
the view. The grit of hammered Oxford under construction.
Matthew Arnold, today, or soon, might be writing his 'Thyrsis'
somewhere or other, about Oxford, 'sweet city with her dreaming
spires'. But in Ada Boyce's 186_, Oxford was anything but static
picturesquerie. Oxford earth was sliced open into canyons, as
foundation pits were sunk in the familiar fields. Oxford air was
thickened with scaffolds for masons working to rival those spires.
Everywhere, Headington limestone folded double upon itself,
yeasting away.

Of course, like many children, Ada was oblivious of the world
in her immediate view. Cowslips and colleges, willows on the
Isis and Cherwell, morning bells rung on the summer wind:
what meant these to Ada? She paid no heed to those inflexible
cows on the other side of the water, standing in Marston fields;
or to that boat on the current, some curate rowing giddy girls
about all on a midsummer's morning. Ada was encased in the
husk of Ada, which consisted, largely, of these: parents distracted
and obscure; Miss Armstrong, not obscure enough, in fact screechy,
bothersome and all too adjacent; and the new Boy Boyce, with

his tiny boyness perched between his legs. Ada wished it might fly away. Or sting itself. Quite hard.

She climbed a stile, huffing and grunting. *Grace* is not a word that comes to mind when Ada lurches into view. But this morning, Ada sacrificed any hopes for proper comportment in order to put a distance between herself and the Bickerage, as she called the Vicarage of Saint Dunstan's.

She paused at a spinney of juvenile ashes. She held her breath a moment to be able to hear over her own exertions. Was that a cry from Miss Armstrong, requiring Ada to halt? Ada wouldn't halt, of course, but it might seem more like fun if she were being chased.

Only the sound of church bells, Christ Church perhaps. Descants of sonorous bronze coin. Falling, falling; where did they pile up? But this is not a question Ada asked herself.

CHAPTER 4

How hateful Miss Armstrong was. 'Pitiable,' Ada's father would have suggested, as a more suitable, a more *benign* adjective. But Ada thought of *hateful* as a scientific term: 'The Hateful Nanny', and so on, **See page XXIX**. A steel engraving in the marginalia might depict Miss Armstrong's distended nostrils and gaspy mouth, marked as *Fig. A.*

Oh, but Miss Armstrong. A highly strung martinet, smelling of lavender and camphor. She once struck the Vicar's wife as not unlike a comic illustration from the pages of the latest number of *Punch,* and so Mrs Boyce had made the mistake of muttering 'Miss Armstrong Headstrong' in Ada's hearing. But the child could have no notion of the battery of affronts that this governess catalogued nightly, after her prayers. On many a grim morning, Miss Armstrong reviewed her trials as she repaired the threadbare lacing of a severe bonnet. *Stitch,* for the times the Reverend Everard Boyce neglected to say good morning on the stairs. *Stitch double stitch,* for the times Mrs Boyce dropped her walking stick and it had to be picked up rather than left lame on the floor where it had fallen. Picked up and repositioned, only to fall again. *Three stitches* and a *prick* of the pin for the tedium of overseeing Ada Boyce, a child parcelled out by a lapse in heaven's supervision, as far as Miss Armstrong was concerned. The guarded eye in that child. That torso. When other girls of Ada's age were gleeful English roses on swaying stems, Ada was a glum, spastic heifer. Sooner or later she'd require a wheeled chair. Miss Armstrong hoped to be well on her way to a new position by the time this happened to Ada. Otherwise the governess might guide such a chair along the banks of the Cherwell and accidentally give it a mighty shove.

No, Miss Armstrong would never stoop to murder. Certainly not. To conceive a crime was not to commit one. Miss Armstrong was aware that imagination, often a cause of temptation and unrest, could also serve the soul: it provided images of morbid behaviour to which one might practise resistance.

A reservoir of resistance: she had built up a huge fund. She needed it.

Miss Armstrong suffered a complaint common amongst staff engaged in homes rich in rectitude though meagre in physical comforts. She felt overlooked as a woman. Of sisterly company there was, effectively, none. (Ada didn't count.) Reverend Boyce's wife, frankly, would have been considered disreputable had Miss Armstrong been one to gossip. (Had the governess anyone to gossip with. Wolverhampton was a long way from Oxford.) But consider: a Vicar's wife, lounging about with her morning robe opened onto terraces of unabashed bosom! Miss Armstrong observed, she didn't comment, she wiped her own nose dry, tightened her own corset. In the matter of Mrs Boyce and dipsomania, Miss Armstrong had perfected a look of restraint and kept her distance as she could.

The governess was grateful not to be homely. Her own colour was as good as her references. But it made no difference. The pious rector treated Miss Armstrong as if she were made of bamboo or clay. As she stood aside in the vestibule when he came in from haunting the parish poorhouse, he all but hung his scarf upon her forearm. Miss Armstrong sometimes tried to communicate her yearning for recognition as a feminine entity by the tilting of an eyebrow. This was too obscure a hieroglyphic for the Vicar to decipher, no matter how Miss Armstrong concentrated the pure fire of her being in the muscles of her forehead. One day she would self-immolate, like Krook in *Bleak House*. Spontaneous combustion caused by an eyebrow left to smoulder a moment too long.

Ada could know none of this, of course, but in cooler moments Ada saw Miss Armstrong clearly enough. Severe, knobby, left-handed, Chapel rather than Church, chiding and churlish by turns, pliant only where Ada's father was concerned. Untapped fervours.

The girl tried to be patient. Vexing though the new baby was proving to be, he might thrive long enough to require a governess. He might pivot Miss Armstrong's attentions away from Ada. Currently the infant had a wet nurse, a nanny, and a steady visitation of doctors, who all thought something might be achieved for the boy, eventually. Or that's what they said. If it lived.

But enough of Miss Armstrong and the dreadful baby. Ada is outside, alone: she is scraping against life the way her brother is. She is newly in the world.

CHAPTER 5

Had Ada known anything of painting, she might have approved of the view before her as a suitable subject for Constable. A vitality in the clouds suggested muscular air, though just now the riverside poplars stood still, as if holding their breath. The world pauses for royalty and deformity alike, and sometimes one can't tell the difference.

Oxfordshire was not *very* like Essex or Suffolk, of course. But Ada was not thinking of Constable and rural English landscapes, but of Hell, and how the city of Oxford, its edges braided with rivers and its atmosphere close and clammy at times, was comfortably unlike Hell.

Since the arrival of her brother, Ada had become better educated in the atmospherics of the underworld. On the night of the bloody nappy, her parents had grown distracted enough for Ada to get her hands on her father's volume of Dante's *Inferno,* the first French edition of 1861. Ada could read no French but she could understand French pictures. The sensational illustrations were by Doré. They weren't yet popularized in England; this edition had been procured in Paris by some clerical colleague of the Reverend Boyce.

She had pored over the pages of the purloined book. She could glean little of the story of Dante's journey underground. But what a tale the pictures told. Everywhere gloom, and mystery and oddment. Barren landscapes of slag-slope; creatures rare and frightening; and firm-fleshed nakedness throughout. Miss Armstrong, coming athwart Ada, had pounced. She'd impounded the book under her own pillow. She'd declared that worry had deranged the Master and sherry the Mistress, and for the nonce they were unfit to supervise their own children.

But too late. Ada had been vouchsafed a glimpse of the underworld. What glustery, ghastly improbabilities might open up beneath the roots of the Iffley yew, should the Boyces have to dig a grave in the family plot at the Church of Saint Mary for the burial of Infant Male! Ada hoped she might be excused from attending the interment. If any of those scaly-tailed figures were to emerge from the soil, let them grasp Miss Armstrong and drag *her* down, Persephone in Pluto's dirty palace. Miss Armstrong might find a new position, one more to her liking.

Children tread the line between worlds. 'Suffer the little children to come unto me' isn't just the granting of permission, but the announcement of privilege, preferment.

So here we are. On her way to her friend's house, Ada rounded a copse of copper beeches along the riverbank. She came upon Alice's older sister sitting in the shade. Lydia had a big book in her lap. She looked up at Ada, startled. Perhaps lulled by the wind on the water, the morning light in the leaves, Lydia had been about to drowse. 'Oh, you,' Lydia said, with little affection. 'You must be looking for Alice.'

'Must I?' asked Ada. 'I've been sent to deliver a gift of marmalade to the household.'

'I shouldn't go there, were I you. Mr Darwin of great renown is visiting today, and he and Papa are arguing about stuff and nonsense. They sent Alice and me away as they thought us too impressionable. Alice is about somewhere. She was here a moment ago. What is that dreadful odour?'

'It's the opodeldoc. For my rheumatism. What are you reading?' The book was splayed in full view. It featured nothing like the thrilling pictures of Doré. Only paired columns of type. There seemed to be no dialogue.

'You're too young for rheumatism. I should revolt if they tried to rub me with an unguent that nasty. Oh, the book? Papa thrust it at me and told me to read to Alice, but you know Alice. I was trying to do as I was told. The piece is about a Shakespeare play, *A Midsummer Night's Dream*. I doubt you've heard of it.'

'Father deplores the stage. "Vice in Three Acts", he says.'

'Curious. I didn't know there *were* that many acts of vice.' Lydia had fifteen years to Ada's ten, and everything the older girl said sounded as if it meant more than Ada could understand. 'Ah, well. It would be easier to watch this folderol than it is to read about it.' Lydia yawned. 'Alice was here a moment ago. Perhaps she has wandered over to look at the stork nest. You might find her there.' Lydia pointed to some imprecise horizon. 'You know our Alice. She plays hide-and-seek but sometimes forgets to ask someone to look for her.'

'I'll continue on to your house and perform my duty.'

'What a little prig you are. Stay out of Darwin's way or he'll turn you into a monkey. Or maybe an ass.' Lydia flapped one hand at Ada. She turned a page of her book with the other. Then she paused. 'Is someone calling after you?'

'Surely not,' said Ada.

'Is that your governess? What is her name? Miss Armstrong? The tightly sprung woman from *Wolverhampton*?' She made Wolverhampton sound like Purgatory.

'Holy Hell,' said Ada. 'I'll be going now.'

'The language of you young people.' Lydia sighed. So few years on Ada, yet such opportunity for condescension. 'Hide-and-seek, you too? I may pretend to be dozing so as not to have to speak to your governess. Though I suppose in any case she will sniff you out. Your medicinal cologne.'

Ada didn't reply. She hurried to the other side of the tree, where a companion tree joined it at the ankle. The pair leaned out over the water, and Ada tried to lean along with them so they would conceal her. The double trunk split into tuberous roots, forming a proto-Gothic archway in the sandy bank just inches above the river. From that join, Ada saw a nose and then a face emerge, twitching. A denizen of the riverbank worried himself out. Adjusting his waistcoat and standing erect, he turned this way and that. He seemed not to notice Ada. She was in the shadows. She didn't dare call out to Lydia for fear she would startle the creature, but really: a white rabbit in a gentleman's waistcoat! Who could possibly have run up that snug apparel and struggled him into it?

'Miss Lydia,' called Miss Armstrong, brisking along the path that meandered towards the riverbank from the outcrop of distant homes. 'I was to accompany Miss Ada on her perambulations, but she left the Vicarage before I was ready. I am quite cross with her.'

Ada didn't dare move. She watched Lydia expertly drop her head back upon the grassy bolster as if in slumberland. Good. She would not give Ada away. Ada leaned further along the slant of the trees, trying to become more shadow-covered. The rabbit had hopped a few feet towards the sunlight, but at the sound of Miss Armstrong's voice he froze. 'The time has got away from me,' cried Miss Armstrong, 'I couldn't locate my gloves. Miss Lydia, is Ada about? Have you seen her?' Then her voice dropped; she had noticed Lydia's closed eyes. 'Beg pardon,' whispered Miss Armstrong, and turned this way and that, as if sniffing for Ada.

All at once Ada found that she'd stepped into the rabbit-hole. If she didn't get loose, she'd be stuck here, clenched by soil and tree-root, pounced upon by her persecutrix. She put the marmalade jar in the pocket of her pinafore and reached down to dig her foot out. Though mere inches from the river, the sandy soil was dry and easily shovelled away. Still, bending at the waist was hard labour for Ada. Before she could retract her ankle, a sub-flooring of rotted root-mass gave way. She was in as far as her knee. She knelt, she had no choice, and she scrabbled at the yielding earth. She was swallowed up by the ground, just as she had hoped would happen to Miss Armstrong in Iffley churchyard. She found herself falling into darkness.

CHAPTER 6

Another curious thing happened then.

A month ago Ada had noticed that she was outgrowing her iron corset, that penitential vest intended to tame the crookedness in her spine. Due to the fuss around her mother's troublesome pregnancy and the wretched offspring it produced, a new device had yet to be fabricated. Now, as Ada fell, the contraption underneath her outer clothes sprang open of its own accord. Ada was accustomed to such relief only in the bath or in dreams. How could the cord slip free from the grommets while she tumbled? The articulated halves of her portable prison were ripping through the cotton husking of her clothes. The appendages flapped behind her. Tatters of fabric – her camisole, her chemise – rippled. She was so shocked at the sense of liberty that it took her a moment to notice that this was a tumble without a stop.

In time – and when does a fall take time, except for the drift of a leaf or a snowflake, or perhaps a lapse into perdition? – Ada's attention turned to her plight. She was dropping down the middle of a cylindrical shaft shaped like a very long, very clean smoke-stack. What furnace but the fires of Hell might require such a column? In any event, all ought to have been Stygian darkness if she'd sunk more than a yard from the tree roots. But a pellucid gleam struck the walls at regular intervals. She couldn't tell where the subtle light came from. It seemed inherent rather than solar.

The sides of the vertical tunnel were paved neatly in Cotswold stone. This shaft must have taken labourers seven years to build, she guessed. Goodness, but it was lengthy. Perhaps she had slipped into some sort of sleeve inside a wheel-rim that went all the way around the globe, under the surface of the world, and joined up with itself in an endless circuit. The wheel that made the world turn. Eventually she would meet up with the hole she had first slipped into. Maybe she'd pop out again, head-first like that rabbit. Or maybe, while she was making her orbit, workers were sealing the breakage. When she reached the spot she'd entered, it would just be more stone, more brick. No doorway out. She'd fall forever and never land. She'd be the world's first internal asteroid.

Or what if she actually was dropping straight down, and would come out in the Antipodes? She might have to learn to walk on her hands. It could scarcely be harder than balancing on her feet, she supposed. Balance, as Miss Armstrong often reminded Ada, was a gift from the Lord to those who deserved it.

She heard a distant scream. Not terrified, but startled. Was it some screech she had made herself, an echo still ricocheting along the walls? Ada couldn't tell from which direction the sound had come. Might it be, perhaps, Alice? Was she here, too? If so, had she already fallen, or was she above Ada, just starting her descent?

Nothing to be done about it now, but wait till they met up. If they did.

She began to notice alcoves in the stonework. Some of them had been used as shelves. She must be falling more slowly than she thought, for by training herself to concentrate, Ada could make out some of the items. A candle snuffer like the one she'd once smuggled outside, in an attempt to catch a minnow while Miss Armstrong was lost in rue. Ada had dropped it in the water.

How had it ended up here? Well, *down* here? And then a row of books. They looked suspiciously like those astringent volumes that Miss Armstrong had tried to read aloud until, one by one, Ada had misplaced them under sofa cushions or in the fireplace. Why, there was *The History of the Fairchild Family*! Ada recognized the scuffed bands on the spine of brown roan. How Miss Armstrong had shivered over the moral depravity exhibited by little lisping Henry, Emily and Lucy Fairchild. Surely Ada had lost *that* book, thoroughly, in the grate? She'd stood there for some time, poking the pyre of coals so that no evidence of her own corruption survived to thrill her governess.

Ada was now falling so languorously that the book was within her reach. She could grab it to see if her name was written in the flyleaf. But she left it where it was. Should she be falling into Hell, she wouldn't be surprised to see *The History of the Fairchild Family* as a set text for the instruction of the juvenile damned. She felt she could almost quote her father's favourite passage. The one where pious Mr Fairchild takes his sin-weakened children to see a corpse hanging on a gibbet. 'The body of a man hung in chains; it had not yet fallen to pieces, although it had hung there some years. It had on a blue coat, a silk handkerchief round the neck, with shoes and stockings and every other part of the dress still entire; but the face of the corpse was shocking, that the children could not look upon it. "When people are found guilty of stealing, or murder, they are hanged upon a gallows . . . till the body falls to pieces, that all who pass by may take warning by the example."' Ada felt she could wait a while longer to meet this passage anew, and so she left the book where it was.

If she truly *were* falling in some sort of circuit, vast or immediate, she would pass this location again. Why shouldn't she place something else here and see if she came across it later? That would prove circularity of a sort. Should she leave behind her corset? No – while it had sprung free like an open trap, tearing her clothes, its iron webbing was still affixed to her arms. Perhaps the jar of marmalade in the pocket of her pinafore? Very well. If she deposited it here without delivering it to Alice's family at the Croft, it would become something she'd stolen. It would belong in this treasury of ill-gotten goods. So, soon enough, *voilà,* an empty ledge. As she reached to put the jar on the shelf, though, she dropped it. It fell more swiftly than she did, disappearing beneath her in the ill-lit gloom. She didn't hear anything like a smash, or anyone crying out, 'Oy! Watch it up there!' Oh well. Marmalade has to make its own way in life, like the rest of us, she thought.

What with her tormented spine, she'd never been allowed to swim. She wondered if this was the time to try. She raked her limbs. She only succeeded in inching her corset further off her arms. It wouldn't come off unless she undressed herself almost entirely. If I am headed to Hell, where's the harm, she thought. According to Doré, everyone is naked there. She wriggled out of her pinafore and then her smock and her torn chemise. The back brace, which often rubbed her raw despite the shift that she wore underneath it, began to clink and clatter. Twisting in the air, like Jacob wrestling with the angel, Ada managed to remove one arm from the iron sleeve-hole. The second arm slipped out much more easily. 'Goodbye!' she said to the device as it arched its grommety iron spine and extended its ribs. It took to solo flight. It didn't fall as she fell, but began to rise. Soon it was out of sight. What that sourpuss Lydia would think of the iron brace emerging from the rabbit-hole without its cargo of twisted child, Ada couldn't begin to imagine. Up until ten minutes ago, Ada had not had much experience in the practice of imagination.

She was dropping faster. Since she was now falling face forwards, she saw that she was catching up with the marmalade jar. Shortly she reached it and snatched it out of the air. Now she *would* store it, and see if it showed up again. Upon the next ledge she came across, two mice were larking about. They were dressed in blue denim caps and chewing on stems of grass. As if they'd been expecting her for most of eternity, they accepted the jar of marmalade she thrust their way with brisk, businesslike nods. One of them winked. The other tipped his cap. 'It's meant for the Croft,' she told them, in case they were going towards Alice's house. However, Alice's house was home to that wicked cat, Dinah, so perhaps mice would be unwilling to make deliveries to that particular larder.

Would she see the marmalade again, and the *Fairchild Family*? Would her flying corset come sweeping towards her from below? If so, that would be proof she was falling in an endless circle. She'd have to take up a hobby of some sort if she were to fall for eternity.

Would she become lonely? Now there was an interesting question. She'd never been alone long enough to imagine what being lonely might be like. Perhaps she'd have the chance to try. She might even like it.

Before she could decide whether or not she was pleased at this possibility, her fall ended suddenly. Not in a bloody splatter, as she might have feared had she got around to thinking about it, but in a shattering splash. Salt water closed over her head before she knew what was happening. A liquid ceiling divided her from the crepuscular tunnel above. Her eyes closed of their own accord. Gone were the mice, and marmalade, and much else she had not yet had a chance to examine closely.

Death, Ada's father had begun recently to insist, comes to us all.

CHAPTER 7

Lydia. The sister who sits and reads in a book 'with no pictures and no conversation'.

Lydia's charade of napping has worked. Her eyelids are aware of a blond blur, a diffusion of sunlight. Miss Armstrong, the pinch-nosed spinster from the Vicarage, has passed by, hastening through the grass.

Having let the volume fall closed, Lydia leaves it like that. It pinches her finger. She doesn't mind if she loses her place. She has only the dimmest sense of what Shakespeare is on about in *A Midsummer Night's Dream*. Yet, almost against her will, Lydia has begun to absorb a notion proposed by the essayists. Shakespeare's farrago of a comedy, they suggest, is a series of nested stories. The maestro Shakespeare wants the theatregoer to see them as if cupped one within the next, or at least contiguous: a royal couple at their leisure; the court of magical Titania and Oberon and fierce Puck; the rustics practising for their crude theatrical; the performance of that sketch itself, which is another world. Does it go further in? Lydia has lost track.

As she lolls in a state of sleep-like abandon (it is not sleep, it is not a dream), Shakespeare's embedded narratives begin to merge and overlap. Does the lion played by Peter Quince have any significance to Puck? Do Puck's tricks matter in the lives of Theseus and Hippolyta, crowned heads of Athens? Does

Shakespeare matter to a pubescent girl? Lydia, Lydia, one hip nudging the bole of a tree, half sprawled on sweet summer grass.

She almost dozes. The degrees of difference between sleep and wakeful alertness are multiple. The closed book makes a papery mouth upon her hand.

Now her thoughts jostle, like blossoms in a vase, blossoms that someone has cupped with her palms, to refresh; but has gone away again. The same flowers, the same thoughts, in nearly but not exactly the same arrangement as before.

Instead of that Elizabethan rigmarole, Lydia's mind stutters towards her own mid-Victorian world. She is dimly aware of invisible systems and enterprises that hold her and all whom she knows. Categories. She doesn't name them for she isn't an ency-clopaedist: indeed, if she turned her full attention to this sidelong thought, it would evaporate. But we can guess, we can glean.

The *dramatis personae*, first. Her father is a failed scholar. Mr Clowd is cerebral and uncertain, groping in a world of shattered statues. Armless blind maidens, unmanned kouroi. Lydia suspects he suffers the temptation towards Rome, as this year he has dragged his family through the broken arches of dissolved monas-teries. Yet he is at the same time a distant friend of Darwin, through the Thomas Huxley connection – Huxley an outlier cousin of some sort. Lydia's father worries over the scandalous notion of natural selection with appalled fascination. In politics he claims no allegiance; he has become inured to Whig and Tory alike. Lately he's been known to stay up all night in the kitchen and bake himself a pie. Mrs Brummidge was no end of startled when she found him one morning over the Kitchener range, floured to the elbows.

Lydia is old enough to picture her father dispassionately, or so she thinks. The pockety skin afore his ears, where he makes a hopeless attempt to trim his own sideburns. The spectacles always askew because, it seems, one ear is higher than the other.

He is tall and scant of hair except on his chin and cheeks. From a distance he has the appearance of a walking cucumber that has gone deliquescent in the middle. He has always been cheerful to his daughters if distracted of late.

Darling Mama within her own moments. In Lydia's dozing mind we must allow only present tenses; there is no backstory in dream. Time slips all its handcuffs.

So: airs and portents for Mama. Scandals implied and denied in a single gesture involving the shoulder and the wrist. Mesmerism. An obscure form of what in a few decades will come to be known as aestheticism, though Mama's skirmishes towards beauty involve ecstatic poetry and plumes of drying marsh grass. She adores Lydia, is baffled by Alice, and never lets on that she is aware the neighbours call the girls the Iceblock Sisters, for the hydrocephalic proportions of their skulls. What are we learning? That this family is a family of courtesies, and secrets. But so is every family. The girls have overheard the titters, the muttered phrases meant to redden their ears. They've pretended to believe their mother hasn't heard them, too. They walk on, Mama in front with her hands folded, her daughters tottering along behind with their heads, like under-set puddings, wobbling as if they might tumble.

And Alice, ah, Alice. But Alice is largely missing from Lydia's thoughts.

Lydia has begun to dream of other networks of thought. They interpenetrate and interrupt, like great angled dials of diaphanous webbing. Faith and its horrors. The furtive lore of sex. The quirkish worlds of Andersen and Hoffmann and the unexpurgated Chaucer. It might as well be Puck, and Nick Bottom, and Oberon and Titania, and Hermia and Lysander: coordinates superimposed one upon the other, in this netherworld of not-quite-dream-not-yet-waking . . . until Lydia is hooked homewards by the sound of a hawking voice.

'Miss Lydia, I beg your pardon. I am disturbing your studies.'

She had let down her guard; she opened her eyes. She regretted it at once. Again, that dreadful governess from the Vicar's house, cantering along the path. In accord to the laws of propriety as they pertain to servants, Lydia allowed a cool, cerebral, 'Miss Armstrong.'

Miss Armstrong had to catch her breath before replying. Lydia was already forgetting her daydreams. She was aware of the bright stamp of sunlight on the sky behind the trees. And Miss Armstrong a grotesquerie, a foreshortened ogress looming overhead.

Lydia sat up, thinking: it is like a tree, is it not, this business of *position*. I am like a squirrel in a tall tree. I have no squirrel words for how high the tree is or how to name my particular perch, but I know my relative position precisely. It is a good deal lower than Pater's, because he is the paterfamilias. Pater is lower than Darwin. Darwin in all his genius idiosyncrasy is nonetheless lower than the Queen. I am, however, on a higher branch than Miss Armstrong, despite her superior years. We both recognize that.

'How lucky for me, you're awake. Where might Alice be?' asked Miss Armstrong.

Ah, Alice, thought Lydia. Now, of children and *their* whereabouts, it is harder to speak. 'Good morning, Miss Armstrong.'

Lydia's courtesy was cutting. Miss Armstrong flushed. 'You must forgive me. I have forgotten my manners. Good morning, Miss Lydia. You are keeping well, I trust?'

'You're looking for Alice?' asked Lydia. Rudeness to a servant from another household was unbecoming; Lydia had lost a little of her ranking. She made up for it. 'You're out of breath, Miss Armstrong. Would you care to pause for a moment?' How careful, that *for a moment*.

'I mustn't interfere with your meditations.' She opened her

palm upon her waist in a casual way. 'In actual fact, I wasn't really looking for Alice.'

'Very wise,' said Lydia. 'Alice isn't easy to pin down. She was here a few moments ago. We've been sent out of the house. Perhaps to escape contagion by blasphemy. Pater has several visitors, one of them a certain Mr Darwin.' She looked up to see if Miss Armstrong registered the name of Mr Darwin. Miss Armstrong didn't seem to appreciate the outrageous prestige of such a visitor.

'Actually, it is our Ada I require,' said Miss Armstrong. 'The new lord of the family is fretful this morning, so Ada and I were to pay a call on your household and contribute a token of esteem. A jar of Mrs Boyce's Seville marmalade. Ada left the Vicarage before I had found my gloves.'

Lydia yawned.

'But Ada isn't generally allowed to wander the riverbanks alone, what with her—' Miss Armstrong looked into the hems of both gloves, as if the acceptable description of Ada's monstrousness were stitched thereupon. 'Her condition,' she concluded.

'Ada is able to move about quite well on her own,' observed Lydia.

'Or so she *thinks*,' said Miss Armstrong darkly. As if Ada were an amputee who hadn't yet cottoned on to the fact that walking was out of the question. 'At any rate, I tiptoed past you here on my way to the Croft. Your cook said that Ada hadn't been seen there today, so perhaps she'd met up with Alice on the riverbank. And Alice would be with you, she said. So I've returned to find Alice, and I hope Ada with her.'

Lydia looked about theatrically. 'Alice is missing. Generally.'

'That is unkind. Ada has her struggles, and Alice has hers. And so do you and I.'

Lydia didn't want to be part of a compound subject conjoined with Miss Armstrong. 'I don't know where Alice is. She was kicking last year's chestnuts into the water a while ago but has run off. It's true that Ada came by as I was reading, but I didn't see in which direction she headed. I'm sure the girls met up, and are larking about.'

'Ada doesn't *lark*. It's not in her nature. And she hasn't the strength.'

'Well, then,' said Lydia, shrugging.

CHAPTER 8

Who first, upon sensing the backward rush of memory said to signal the moment of death, was able to telegraph this apprehension to the family gathered around? Maybe the original gentleman descended from ape said the equivalent of 'falling out of tree' to his common-law ape wife, and she interpreted his words as 'just as he left for the dusty world beyond, his whole life passed before his eyes. Then he hit the ground.' After all, falling out of the tree is the first and the last thing we do.

And what might death seem like for those prior to language? Infants, say. Or for those incapable of memory, the simple folk known as God's beloveds? What can the final moments be like for humans who are now beyond both language and memory, like certain great-aunts in bonnets that went out of fashion a half-century ago?

For Ada, who was only a decade old, the memories came as illustrations in books. She saw first a dense and beautifully crisp illustration from that collection of Doré's engravings for *The Inferno*: specifically, **Plate 10** from Canto III, Charon supervising the embarkation of sinners in a boat on a dark lake. Unlike Ada, the sinners were magnificent human specimens, swollen into adult sensuousness with citrus-round breasts, if female, and mathematically beautiful abdomens and buttocks, if male. Without complaint the damned must have worn their iron spines in childhood, to die with such correct posture. Still, it wasn't the divine bodies of sinners that Ada now recalled, but the netherworld itself. Beyond the slopes of scree, Doré had limned a black sky pasted across with blacker, underground clouds. The landscape looked like certain sections of Cumberland she'd seen once on a family mission of mercy to an ailing great-aunt near Coniston. ('No rest for the Vicar'd,' her father had muttered.) But Ada couldn't figure out Doré's sky under the earth, a sky that wasn't a heaven. It must be a holy mystery, to borrow a phrase from Cook. Or a damned mystery.

Twisting deep within the Lake Amniosis into which she had fallen, her mind flipped some page backwards, to other illustrations she had seen. Because less pertinent, perhaps, to her effort of dying, they were less clearly apprehended. Some blotty woodcuts of *The Rational Brutes; or Talking Animals,* by Dorothy Kilner. The frontispiece from *Goody Two-Shoes,* published once upon a time at John Newbery's shop. Though it more often served the cause of mirth, that greasy volume had been passed down through her mother's family for the instruction of several generations already. One might live out an uplifting, book-length life if one was lucky. Or out-live one, if one was luckier. (***The Short Life and Inspiring Death of Ada Boyce: Presto to Finis, with Hand-tinted Woodcuts for Instruction and Delight, etc.***)

The oldest picture Ada could recall was a representation of Noah's Ark, on a page stained with oatmeal. Earlier than that she could not remember.

Drifting underwater, Ada felt as if she must have missed the Ark, along with the unicorns and behemoths and centaurs and other failed species. She was doomed to extinction any minute now. In the picture as she recalled it, bearded Noah looked like her reverend father, making no effort to notice his daughter flailing beneath the waves. Her mother was below-decks with her chin in an Old Testament chalice of Madeira. There was no Cook on board the Ark as far as Ada knew; Ireland hadn't been invented yet. She had a suspicion that Noah's newborn infant son had trotted along on all fours and tripped up his big ungainly sister, making her sprawl and tumble overboard into the flood. Sororicide.

Then, to her surprise, she broke through.

But broke through what? It seemed, at least, to be the surface of the water. Perhaps more. As in the landscape by Doré, an impossible, outlandish sky lolled overhead with an unsettling suggestion of eternity.

She was naked. But she suspected she hadn't been made corporeally perfect in her plunge.

'I say,' called a voice, 'I do hope you're not drowning.'

She looked about for a boat, for Noah and his Ark, for Charon and his barque, anyone on duty. She saw no boat, but as she pivoted – how much easier it was to move in water than on land! – she discovered that she was close to a strand. A couple of peculiar-looking creatures were making their way along the beach, from left to right. A Walrus walking hand in hand with a labourer of some sort. A difficult thing to accomplish, given that walruses sport nothing approximating a hand. Still, there was no other way to put it. The human had some obscure tools of his trade poking from a pocket in his labourer's leather apron.

Neither of them looked like Charon. Nor like Noah. Perhaps the human, who seemed to be a joiner, had learned shipbuilding from Noah, whilst the Walrus had survived the flood because, of course, walruses swim adequately enough.

'I may be drowning,' she called.

'Please don't,' came a reply. They had stopped and were peering at her. The Walrus was speaking. 'We just saw a sign that said DROWNING IS FORBIDDEN AND PUNISHABLE BY DEATH.'

'The Queen is ruthless about misbehaviour of that sort,' added his companion.

'If one drowns, one can't then be put to death,' said Ada. She polliwogged nearer the shore, keeping her bare shoulders submerged.

'I don't know why you say that. One can drown one's sorrows in a flask of herring cordial, but the sorrows always return,' said the Walrus. 'They don't stay drowned. They can be put to death again happily enough.'

He was a Walrus who looked as if he knew something considerable about sorrow. Then again, thought Ada, perhaps most walruses look like that.

'Why is an oyster like a writing desk?' asked the tradesman.

'Ah. My friend,' said the Walrus to Ada, 'is a Carpenter, and he knows many useful things about writing desks. As we are just returning from a breakfast with oysters, perhaps he intends to write about it.' To the Carpenter, the Walrus said, 'An excellent riddle, my dear man. The very wet child beyond may have an opinion on the matter.'

'Why is an oyster like a writing desk?' called the Carpenter in a voice keyed to falsetto.

Ada had found purchase with her feet now, so she could stop rotating her arms and knees. She said musingly, '*Why* is an oyster like a writing desk?'

'That's *our* riddle,' remarked the Walrus. 'Don't ask it back to us. You can ask us one of your own. If you have one.'

'I'm pondering. Why is an oyster like a writing desk?' She reviewed the conversation they'd had. 'I think I know. An oyster is like a writing desk because neither can be drowned.'

'That's the correct answer,' said the Walrus. He drooped his moustache further than usual. 'You're good.'

'Do I get a prize?' asked Ada. 'Where I come from, riddles are sometimes tests to prove the merit of the hero. If the hero guesses the answer correctly, very often a door is opened unto him.'

'Well, if a hero comes along, we'll open the door for him,' said the Walrus. 'That's your prize.'

'And if there isn't a door, I'll build one,' said the Carpenter. 'Do you have a riddle for us?'

Ada only knew one riddle. 'When is a door not a door?'

The pair of beachcombers looked at each other from beneath whiskery eyebrows. The Walrus shrugged. 'It is a dreadful mystery,' whispered the Carpenter. 'No one can *ever* know the answer to that question. It is existentially, hyperbolically, quintessentially unknowable.'

'I know it, and I'll tell you,' said Ada proudly. 'A door is not a door when it is ajar.'

'A jar of what?' asked the Walrus. 'Jellyfish jam, I hope? Mackerel marmalade?'

'No, *ajar* – it's a word that means *open*. Standing open.'

The Carpenter slapped his palm against the Walrus's upturned flipper, and they danced a bit of a quadrille, as well as they could without six partners.

'Well, that settles that, then!' said the Carpenter. 'Am I right or am I right?'

'Is that another riddle?' asked Ada. 'What do I get if I answer it correctly?'

'A further chance to fail,' said the Carpenter. He stopped cavorting and the two of them began to trudge away. Oyster shells, the ones that had fallen from their pockets as they danced, cracked when trod upon. They made a sound like the splintering of fine porcelain.

When the pair of ambassadors had passed from view, and Ada couldn't see another creature about, she clambered out of the salt sea. The air was cool on her skin. Her clothes waited on the strand, dry and neatly folded. They showed no sign of damage. A sprig of seaweed was attractively arranged upon the top like a spray of rosemary. Ada dressed with little pain and an ease that approached the gymnastic. The sensation was so novel as to be nearly troubling. Once appropriately clothed, she walked along the sand in the direction from which her interlocutors had come. She didn't care to encounter them again, at least not just yet. She wasn't sure why. Her gait was still lopsided, but so was the world, so she kept on.

CHAPTER 9

It seemed there was nothing to be done but that Miss Armstrong must sit down. Lydia would be spared the essay analyzing Shakespeare's comedy. Trying not to feel grateful to Miss Armstrong about that, Lydia made the briefest of nods. The gesture was an unconscious imitation of her mother's, once upon a time.

Lacking awkward crinolines, Miss Armstrong collapsed to the grass with a flump. Yes, Lydia thought: as the poet contends, God's in His heaven – All's right with the world. The hillside's dew-pearled and slightly greasy. The governess's skirts will be creased, quite probably stained, she noted with satisfaction. She allowed herself to say, 'I'm certain Ada Boyce is lurching about somewhere.'

'Oh, yes, well. *Somewhere,*' said Miss Armstrong dolorously, waving her arms. She looked alarmed. 'I can hardly return to that – that *place* – with the news that I've lost track of her. I shall be let go if I am seen to have let *her* go.'

'I expect you are referring to the Vicarage. How is Boykin Boyce getting on?'

'Assessments differ, but in any case, the little prince is croupy. That means Cook is unpleasant, and Ada is unpleasant, and Mrs Boyce is—' She jumped over the treacherous gulf of that unspoken remark and landed on the other side. Which proved a still more perilous terrain. 'And the Master of the house is my *bête noire,*

Miss Lydia.' But Miss Armstrong hadn't meant to utter those words. They'd been spoken from depths she believed to be beyond language. Knowing that she couldn't easily retract them or make them mean other than what they seemed to suggest in mile-high letters, she burst into tears.

Lydia didn't claw for the slip of handkerchief she kept in her pocket. Miss Armstrong would have her own. Sure enough, here it came, useful for blotting the nasal symphonics and the patting of eyelashes gone gluey in a monsoon of feeling sufficient to dampen all Rangoon. 'Miss *Armstrong*. If you please.'

That was all that was needed. Miss Armstrong regained her bearings as if she'd been arrested by a constable and brought before a magistrate under charges of public incoherence.

'My, my. I don't know what came over me, Miss Lydia. Perhaps the crying of Baby Boyce has become infectious. He's a right little runtling, he is.'

Lydia, having caught the thread, was inclined to pull it. 'Tell me about your Reverend Everard Boyce,' she said. 'I've hardly been introduced.' The *your* was salt salt salt.

'I'm sure I don't gossip.' Despite the testimony, Miss Armstrong looked entirely unsure.

'From a distance, the good Reverend Boyce cuts a fine figure.'

'Oh, well, if it is figures you want, take up skating on ice.' Miss Armstrong, proud of the riposte, straightened her spine.

'Is it true that Mrs Boyce repaired to her chamber after the happy event and that she refuses to emerge?'

'From whom would you have heard such calumny? Yes, it's true.'

'Which must put a certain pressure upon the rest of the household.'

'I am happy to say clockwork could not run more smoothly than at the Boyce establishment.'

'But the poor Vicar. I hope he isn't deprived of his wife's affections.'

'You scandalize me, Miss Lydia.'

'It was not I who burst into tears at his name.'

Miss Armstrong cast her head away. The angle suggested she
had avian forebears. When she relaxed and returned to glance
at Miss Lydia, she said, 'You are a wicked child, to tempt me
towards an allowance of intimacy you've no intention of returning.
My respect for my employer is unbounded, and exactly appropriate to my station and to his. I shall thank you not to return
to the subject.'

Lydia plucked at some grass and petted it as if it were the
forelock of a Tennyson-besotted youth lying in her lap. The tone
she employed was languorous. 'I have known unrequited love.'

Miss Armstrong was stronger than that. 'I suspect there are
few girls of your affectionate nature who couldn't say the same.
Miss Lydia, I am loath to return to the Bickerage – the Vicarage
for the reasons given. I must find Miss Ada. But *your* home is
in a state, your servants busy with the guests who have come to
call on your father. Your Mrs Brummidge said there was a child
in the house but it wasn't Ada.'

'I don't know who that might be. Perhaps the kitchen maid's
sister has come to observe how to do no housework.'

'Do you think there's any possibility Ada could be lurking
about the Croft in the hopes of engaging that visiting child in
play? Ada is lonely, you understand. And your sister can be fickle
about including Ada in the romps of childhood.'

Lydia felt a rare moment of guilt. 'Ada shouldn't consider
herself singled out for snubbing. Our little Alice often lives in
her own world.'

'She's not alone in that practice.' Miss Armstrong rose and
smoothed her skirts as best she could. Yes, grass stains a-plenty,
but they didn't fill Lydia with the glee she'd anticipated. 'If you
have no recommendation on where I might find either of them,
Alice or Ada, I shall continue to look on my own. But if Ada

should come by, would you ask her to wait with you until I return? I shall be sure to pass by on my way home.'

'I may not still be here.'

'I wouldn't hold you here on my account.' She gazed along the riverbank in the direction of the University Parks, Christ Church Meadow, and beyond that Iffley, Bournemouth, Majorca, Patagonia. 'I suppose it's possible that, giddy in her liberation, Ada decided to go see the Iffley yew. It's a popular destination for those on a mission of picnic. I only hope she hasn't slipped in the water and fetched up against the milldam.' She set out with a purpose, but turned when Miss Lydia called her name.

'Miss Armstrong,' said Lydia, smiling with a contemptuous vagueness, 'you mustn't fret. Your secret is safe with me.'

'My secret?' said Miss Armstrong in a rush, as if she had revealed something sinister about milldams and damp-ruined children. Then, remembering her admission about Everard Boyce, she blushed a rogue scarlet.

Lydia settled back into the arms of the tree, and Shakespeare, and the lost romantics in the forests around Athens.

CHAPTER 10

Perhaps she dozed a little. It was that kind of an early summer day. In dreams, time may eddy and distort, but even when it traffics in the past, it does so in the guise of the present moment.

No breeze stirs. Water in slow motion. The glop of a tench breasting for a dead beetle. The river, so slow and murmurous as nearly to be mute, sealing the wound. The shriek of children at play across the fields, pestering a cow, whose bell makes jaundiced comment as she hustles away. Now a breeze arises. In the subtlest of commotions, poplar leaves shift and touch one another, and subside. A frog out of sorts with its social life croaks, but only once, as if thinking the better of it.

Dreams ride in us, frictionless, dark reflections in bright water.

Against the mutability of dream, the natural laws advocated by our bewigged Enlightenment forebears are powerless. Newton, for instance, insists on gravity and other prohibitions of the physical world, from which (while we are awake) we are never free. But we can fly in dreams.

Other bearded potentates – Jehovah, Cronos, all their ilk – they sort time through their fingers. They never confuse the strands: but dreams play havoc with sequence.

Of course, these days, the accepted sequence is under revision. Six decades and some into the century, though Browning does indeed reassure us God is still in His heaven, Darwin is taking tea in the Croft. Heaven shudders as Cambrian creatures shake mud from their gills, rewriting history. Sequence, and consequence.

Consider this moment. Queen Victoria, newly mourning the death of Albert the Prince Consort, has cast a spell of propriety, sentiment and moral rigour throughout her realm. *Consequentiality.* Lydia will spend her entire life in a nexus of Victorian social understandings too near to be identified by the naked eye, like viruses, or radiation.

At the same time, with ink staining his forefingers, and crumbs from his hard roll upon his lower lip, Karl Marx is hunched over in the Reading Room of the British Library. He frets, and lays dynamite. History has its own evolutionary strategy, towards consequentialities we cannot anticipate.

In 186_, faith is largely put in *structure.* Slice apart cadavers. Dig up Attic Greece. Examine gluey plant cells under magnification. Colour another corner of Africa the geographer's salmon-pink of Empire, and install the new district commissioner in some obscure equatorial colony to the strains of a dark-skinned military band. Everything that exists is *intact.* Look at it. The established Church, with the Queen as its head. Righteous in faith! The British civil service in its first decade of rule of the Asian sub-continent, following the nationalization of the East India Company. Firmly in control. And social life: as rigid as the ironwork supporting the canopies of the great London railway termini – Waterloo, Charing Cross, Paddington – the class system keeps the London poor separate from the gentry. Mostly. Though some systems can be secretly porous, especially in certain neighbourhoods after midnight.

Meanwhile, strictest of all, and affected by everything already mentioned, the rising middle class hold notions of childrearing that are hemmed round with creeds of nation, faith and family. Children are cornered and dragooned even by those who adore them. For their own good. For the good of their characters and their immortal souls.

But what is character? How solid? We cut our hair, we shave our beards, we lose a limb. We remain ourselves. In dreams, however, we swap identities licentiously. We sabotage the structures of our character without a thought.

None of this occurs to Lydia in so many words. A little lost ladybird stumbled into great concentric spider-webs. Yet, as she drowses, sunlight pinking her bared forearms, she nearly wonders, where in all these enterprises of thought and institution is Lydia herself? What is the character of Lydia, and where the soul of Lydia, were there still such a thing as a soul?

And where, for that matter, *is* Alice?

CHAPTER 11

Ada hadn't gone much further along the strand when she came upon a door standing upon a wooden sill. The door was closed cleanly in its framing, but its jamb was unattached to any wall. Possibly a door that had been built in a shop and abandoned upright upon a beach. When is a door not a door?

Ada found it just as handsome and finished on the far side as on the near. Indeed, it was hard to tell if there was an inside or an outside to the thing. She tried the handle, but the door was locked. Then she looked more closely at the knob. Inscribed in tiny letters across the brass bulb, words so small she could just read them:

KEEP OUT.

Nothing would do, then, but to check the knob on the far side of the door. It said:

OUT KEEP.

Well, she thought, Miss Armstrong's favourite words for me are *outlandish* and *outrageous*. If through that door is where the *out* is kept, perhaps I have no business going there.

She stumped on, disgruntled at having been denied entry to a portion of beach she could reach just as well by ignoring the door altogether.

Still, what sort of Hades might this be, if she were barred from certain sacrosanct sections? Maybe it wasn't actually Hell, just hellish?

Around a soft promontory, she came upon a stand of roses prospering in the lee of a stony slope. They tossed their heads in a salt wind. Ada didn't know much about horticulture. That would involve asking questions of Miss Armstrong and enduring her endless answers. On their daily marches, Ada could never spare the breath to gabble. She needed all her strength for walking.

The flowers were quietly talking amongst themselves as she neared them.

Ada had heard of the language of the flowers. Her parents had sent roses to the Croft that time. They had said that roses spoke of sympathy. But Ada hadn't understood that floriology had an actual tongue. In fact, Ada found symbolic language vexing. When Miss Armstrong Headstrong lunged towards a window, claiming that the sun was a golden chariot drowning in a flaming Tyrrhenian Sea, Ada humped across the room after her and saw only an evening sun partly covered by dark blue and orange clouds. On the basis of her inclination to be literal, Ada had had to relinquish her copy of the *Household Tales* of the Grimm brothers. She would find it worryingly fantastical and unscientific, no doubt, and probably pagan, too. Best not to risk it.

'I do so love a day served up like this. It suits my palate,' said the tallest of the rose-trees, flexing her petals, which were a varnished, carmeline pink.

'Days like this, Rosa Rugosa, are a penny a pound,' replied a second, a thorn-pronged cousin nearby whose blossoms were coloured an apoplectic plum. 'Cheap and cheerful, if you like that sort of thing; and, if you'll allow me to say it, common.'

'It's a strain, pretty days,' said a low-limbed third rose-tree, gloomily. 'Frankly, I don't know why we bother.'

'Ninny. We air our blossoms to signify the passion of the

world,' snapped the thorny purple. 'Though what is passion but blood and *sorrow*?'

Ada knew that eavesdropping was very poor form indeed. As she inched closer, she turned her face to the sea so she wouldn't be caught staring. The horizon seemed to be nearer than it had been before.

At the crest of a strong spine about four feet high, the pink-blossomed creature called Rosa Rugosa bobbed. 'You two would complain at being dipped in liquid gold. What's wrong with buttery sunlight and a vivid wind? I've rarely enjoyed a more gratifying light.' She turned her upper leaves, as if opening her hands. 'A day like this nourishes one.'

'Well, Miss Happy Happiness! Such self-satisfaction,' remarked the plum-violet blossom. 'Preening all day, and for what? *I* never would. Wait till a lovesick courtier or a grieving widow comes by and tries to pluck *me*. I'll give them what-for with my thorns. Mark my words, Rosa Rugosa, you're becoming blowsy.'

Rosa Rugosa took no offence, but rotated her sepal neckline the better to spread her pink petals about in the light.

'You're right, Rosinathorn,' said the low-growing third to the second. 'Rosa Rugosa looks like a hoyden behind a shop counter.'

'Of course I'm right,' snapped Rosinathorn. 'She's parked right in front of me, Rosadolorosa; I can hardly see the shoreline for all her primping. I've a good mind to lean forwards and stab her.'

'Oh, why bother?' Rosadolorosa, the third tree, was a no-nonsense confusion of collapsing hoops and canes. Her few petty blossoms were arrayed without conviction on a single drooping spear. The blossoms were meant to be white, Ada thought, but against Rosa Rugosa's pinks, they looked dingy and lacking in starch. 'It's my belief that our lives are stolen from us. Ornamented with pinnate leaves and coloured frills, we exist only as a consolation for others. I don't feel fulfilled. Indeed, some days I scarcely feel at all.'

'If you begin to weep again from some nameless ontological

grief, Rosadolorosa, I'll call for a pruning,' declared dusky Rosinathorn. 'Bad enough I have Little Honeysweet Sunshine to one side. To have the Flower of Death to the other side is more than stem can bear. I'm not sure which of you is worse.'

Ada found arguing roses to be unsettling. It was so like the Bickerage. 'I think you're all lovely, each in her own way,' she said peaceably.

'Horrors! A spy, listening in at our backstairs nattering!' said Rosa Rugosa. 'Attitudes, girls!' She rearranged herself in as relaxed an odalisque's posture as she could, given she was outfitted with woody stems. Ada knew what *that* felt like.

'This is *such* a charade,' muttered Rosinathorn. Her stems brushed against one another, clicking thorns.

Rosadolorosa made no attempt to compose herself, but sagged in the wind like a white shroud dropped upon the sands.

'I never met flowers who could speak,' said Ada.

'You have not yet met us,' said the first. 'I am Rosa Rugosa.'

'I don't mean to be impertinent,' said Ada, 'but can you tell me what you signify? I mean, in the language of flowers?'

The roses exchanged glances. 'Why do you ask?' barked Rosinathorn.

'Some months ago my parents sent roses to the Croft. They told me the flowers conveyed a message. But I don't know flowers. Do different colours signal different messages?'

'Pink is for happiness,' said Rosa Rugosa promptly. '*Tra la la* and all that.'

'Purple red is for passion, but in my experience that usually means pain,' snarled Rosinathorn. 'Come close to my thorns and I'll show you.'

'White is— but why should I signify anything to anyone?' murmured Rosadolorosa vaguely. 'White is the absence of significance.'

The Boyce family had sent the Clowds a bouquet of yellow

roses. Literature, even of roses, remained a mystery. Ada dropped the matter. 'It's a pleasure to meet you. My name is Ada.'

'Was that Ada, did you say?' Rosa Rugosa leaned upon the available breeze; it looked something like a curtsey.

'Or Ardour?' snickered Rosinathorn, with a certain menace.

'Or Adder?' ventured Rosadolorosa. 'The worm, the worm, he comes for us all.'

'Ada. Miss Ada Boyce, of the Vicarage of Saint Dunstan's, Oxfordshire.'

'A very low address,' said Rosa Rugosa, 'if I've never heard of it.'

'Rosa Rugosa has pretensions,' pointed out Rosadolorosa, sniggering. 'Uppity.'

'Isn't it rewarding to have friends of the heart?' asked Rosa Rugosa in a bright, hysterical tone. 'Mine are always having fun with me.' She beckoned Ada with a spray of leaves.

Ada came nearer, but not too near.

'Now, tell us how you like our little patch of heaven,' said Rosa Rugosa. 'Don't you admire it? I'm sure you've never before seen the likes of us.'

'I don't mean to be contrary, but I've been to the Isle of Wight,' said Ada. 'I've seen roses along the beach before.'

'Oh,' said Rosa Rugosa. She sounded insulted, as if perhaps she had thought herself one of a kind. However, she rallied and continued in a sweet diatribe. 'But have roses seen you? You can't be said to have properly established yourself in a place until you have been *seen* there.'

Ada didn't know how to answer this. When she was out in public, passersby sometimes averted their faces, if not out of disgust then, as she preferred to think, out of charity. Perhaps Rosa Rugosa had a point. She turned her face from the roses so as not to give away her sense of disorientation, both at home and here. 'Is it my imagination or is the sea shrinking?'

'There is no sea,' said Rosa Rugosa. 'This is only a very wide salt-water well. May I present my ladies-in-waiting, Rosinathorn and Rosadolorosa?'

'Who died and made you princess? I'm not waiting upon *you,*' said Rosinathorn. 'I just happen to be rooted in the same neighbourhood.'

Rosadolorosa added, '*I'm* waiting for your pink petals to go beige, Rosa Rugosa. If you must know. Death comes to us all. You first, I hope.'

Rosa Rugosa seemed accustomed to the insurrection of her court, if that's what it was. They could get no nearer to her than fate had planted them; anyway, she was the largest and benefited from the best situation. Ada said to her, 'Are you the queen who forbids drowning?'

'If she's a queen, I'm a sack of anthracite biscuits,' snorted Rosinathorn.

'If she's a queen, I'm a hornet with a head cold,' said Rosadolorosa.

Ignoring the rabble, Rosa Rugosa said loftily to Ada, 'I suppose you could call me a princess. The royalty of beauty. While you . . . well, you aren't beautiful at all. Indeed, you're not like any child I've ever seen before.'

'Have you seen many little girls?'

'Never a one.'

'Then I couldn't be like her. There's no one to be like.'

'And indeed you aren't. Couldn't be more different if you tried.'

Ada tried again. 'Have you noticed someone named Alice come along?'

'Let me think,' said Rosa Rugosa. 'No. Rosinathorn, Rosadolorosa, have you seen an Alice?'

Perhaps they didn't know what an Alice was. Rosinathorn and Rosadolorosa refused to reply.

Ada hurried on. 'It's just that – well, if she's here, I seem to have lost her.'

'Perhaps *she* has lost *you*,' said Rosa Rugosa. 'You aren't much in the way of sparkling companionship so far. You're new here, aren't you?'

'I'm sorry that I've intruded,' said Ada. 'I'll just ask that gardener coming along the strand.'

'Gardener?' shrieked Rosa Rugosa. She began to furl her petals. A creature was making his way towards them at a great speed. He was shaped something like a sail, but bothered by a wind that turned him sideways and showed him to be paper-thin. As he drew closer, Ada could see that he was a playing card about her own height. Which meant either he was a large card or she'd become a very little girl. The Ace of Spades, he seemed, on spindly legs. In one hand he carried a flower basket made of wicker, and in the other a spade.

'They *will* choose to live on the outskirts of respectable society, this lot,' he huffed as he drew nearer. 'Stand aside, child, or you'll be flecked with sand as I dig. I assume you want to keep your frock tidy for the afternoon affair.'

'What are you doing?' asked Ada.

'She calls for roses, and roses she must have,' said the Ace of Spades. Strong for a paper creature, he set to work in the sandy soil near the roots of Rosa Rugosa.

'I am being abducted!' shrieked the princess (if indeed she was one, and not just putting on airs). 'Rosinathorn, to arms!'

Rosinathorn smirked as she retracted her jagged backbone.

Ada asked the gardener, 'Who calls for roses?'

'The Queen.'

'Queen Victoria?'

'Whosoever *that* is, she has no standing here. I'm talking about the Queen of Hearts, don't you know,' said the Ace of Spades. 'We ran low in our count of roses, and I am dispatched to swell the population.'

'This is rape, this is plunder,' shrilled Rosa Rugosa. 'Rosinathorn, ready your thorns! Rosadolorosa, strangle this miscreant with your creepers!'

Rosinathorn and Rosadolorosa attempted nothing of the sort, but remained as still and mute as an arrangement upon a tombstone.

The Ace of Spades began to cantilever Rosa Rugosa's root system upon the spade. A fringe of airy brown threads came to light with a scatter of soil.

'Down below, she's dirty as the rest of us,' sniggered Rosinathorn under her breath.

'Come to stay, have you?' the Ace of Spaces asked of Ada.

Ada hadn't yet considered the duration of her visit to this peculiar place. The question made her uneasy. 'I couldn't say,' she replied. 'I started out by looking for a friend.'

'You'll find no friend *here*,' said the Ace of Spades. 'These are a heartless lot, roses. Very selfish. I'd suggest you try the royal family, the Hearts. But they're worse.'

'Replant me at once or I'll tell the Queen you said that!' said Rosa Rugosa.

'You shut your gob or I'll paint you white,' said the Ace of Spades. Rosa Rugosa obeyed, or perhaps she had fainted. The gardener threw the uprooted princess into his wicker carryall. 'Any other volunteers?' The mean-spirited companions were shocked into silence. Rosinathorn shed all her thorns; they dropped to the ground around her. Rosadolorosa went from white to grey. She appeared to have died of grief, instantly. Before Ada could ask if she might join the Ace of Spades, he was hurrying around the promontory in the direction from which she'd come.

CHAPTER 12

She left Rosinathorn and Rosadolorosa. There was nothing she could do for them. If they revive, let them learn to comfort one another with the language of flowers, she thought. Passion and Annihilation in the absence of Happiness. I have Alice to find.

She followed the Ace of Spades. She was just in time to see him arrive at the door in the sand. He located a key tied to a cord that looped through the handle of his wicker basket. He unlocked the door on the OUT KEEP side and went through, slamming it shut behind him. Ada had been calling to him, calling as in a dream, but her voice was small and lost in the wind. By the time she got to the door, it was locked again. When she walked around the door, the Ace of Spades and Rosa Rugosa were nowhere in sight.

She looked out to the horizon, puzzling. The sea was shrinking. The world on the other side of the ocean became visible. She'd always wondered where Noah's flood went when it was done. Now she knew. Underground.

This sea was gurgling with a murky slurp, as if draining into a section of the new London sewers. Everyone said they were such a miracle, those sewers, relegating the Great London Stink to history. Ada didn't know about that, but she was familiar with an ebb tide at the Isle of Wight. She expected a pungency of fish rot. She smelled only opodeldoc. The blur of the incoming

world was a wave of forest, green heads of elm and oak a sort
of leafy spume. I shall be crushed by a marauding wood, she
thought. This did not terrify her. Something outlandish would
be on the other side of that experience, another OUT KEEP, no
doubt.

Still, she made herself rigid in case the force of the green
tide broke all her bones. She didn't want her limbs to be scat-
tered so far apart as to make reassembly difficult. She understood
that personal integrity was a matter of finding the proper cage;
she'd been broken before, yet her iron corset had kept her
contained.

The crowns of the trees reared back on all sides like the heads
of stallions at dressage. The limbs of onrushing trees linked arms.
The sea had become the size of a puddle and it was still shrinking.
Ada peered, hoping that if it disappeared completely she'd be
able to spy the drain. What could be under the underworld? But
when there was hardly more than a cupful of salt water left in
the sand, it resolved itself into the bowl of a teacup set upon a
saucer. Tied to the porcelain handle was a tag. Words were
written upon it.

Ada groaned at the effort of bending, but the groan was only
habit; bending hardly hurt at all. Before she could lift the cup
and saucer from the sand, however, a breeze blew the sand away,
revealing a shiny disk. This turned into the glass top of a rose-
wood table that thrust itself out of a wooden floor much as a
fountain rises when the spigots are first opened. The table grew
to the height of a pergola, elevating the teacup far out of Ada's
reach. In the shade of the closing forest, only a cup of ocean,
and it was over her head.

I ought to be able to see what the tag says, even if it just
says NO BATHING FOR THREE HOURS AFTER LUNCHEON, thought
Ada. Try as she might, she couldn't climb the pedestal of the
table high enough to read the tag through the glass. She looked

about to find some fallen tree limb that she might prop against the tabletop and thereby scale the slope to the glass plateau. Only now did she realize that, though the approaching forests had halted in time to keep from crushing her, they'd come dreadfully close. They'd boxed her into a sort of capacious coffin. And the forest was turning itself inside out. It assumed the look of an attractive bevelled panelling that lined four sides of a windowless salon. She could find only one door in this long, high chamber, the previously isolated door that said KEEP OUT. It was now properly fitted into a wall. Snug, and no doubt still locked.

Overhead, what Ada had thought were intertwining boughs turned out to be a pale green ceiling, done over in a plaster moulding that emulated the fan-vaulting in Brasenose College Chapel. The effect was faintly pietistic. In the centre of the ceiling, the branches twisted themselves into another instruction: DON'T LOOK UP.

CHAPTER 13

There is no earthly reason why I ought to stay here for the benefit of that Miss Armstrong, thought Lydia. If Ada falls into mischief through lack of supervision, her governess will be shown the door. Then that poor woman's struggles over her feelings for the Vicar will be a matter of the past. In any event, it isn't my duty to play watchguard for Ada Boyce. I'm nobody's servant.

So with a determination to be brusque and to enjoy it, she rose to her feet and turned back towards her own home.

The day was continuing warm, indeed warm enough that showers might follow by tea-time. A certain broodiness of cumulus out towards the Cotswolds as Lydia picked her way along the path. She avoided the eyes of strolling summer scholars and Saturday marketgoers, hustling by with their baskets and barrows, as assiduously as they attempted to catch hers.

Pater had said to keep out from underfoot until the guests left. She expected he had *meant* to say, 'Keep Alice away, as she will only ask vexing questions.' Lydia wasn't certain, but in any case, she was hardly dragging Alice back before tea-time. Lydia would slip in through the kitchen garden and disturb no one. If Alice had already come home and was interrupting affairs, Lydia could claim to have become lost with Theseus and Hippolyta in the forests around Athens. Pater would allow that much.

She made her way past the rangy yews and into the kitchen

garden. Upon the margins of the grounds surrounding the house, newer neighbourhoods were encroaching – the elegant terrace houses in the crescents of Park Town were almost visible through the distant phalanx of trees. But, dating from some previous century, the Croft lingered on, lacking style and symmetry. An undistinguished stone farmhouse with halfhearted stucco chipped away in patchwork pieces to reveal glimpses of a frame timber construction, oak beams filled in with a crazy quilt of brick, rubble, stone. The house seemed to list in the sunlight. An effect of irregular eaves, perhaps. The back door was open. Hens were wandering about like ladies at a lyceum tea trying to find their friends before selecting their seats. The dovecote was silent. The heat made doves dozy.

Mrs Brummidge was slapping dough on the pastry table. Great whuffs of flour paled the air. The room reeked of stewed celery and onion broth. 'Thought you was Carter with that brace of hares, I did,' said the cook, wiping straying hairs away from her brow with the front of her wrist. 'But it's the likes of Miss Lydia inspecting the kitchens, no less.' Her tone was less mocking than it may sound. She was, perhaps, a bit intimidated by the young mistress of the house. 'Where's Alice at, then?'

'Isn't Alice at home?'

'If she's not with you, she's missing again. I worried as much to your father this morning, but then I decided she'd gone with you.'

'I expect she's wandered back. Must be loitering somewhere.'

'Miss Lydia, I made a jam tart and left it steaming on the sill; that always draws Alice for a nibble if she's haunting a place. But she's not come around, I notice. Mayhaps the child has taken Dinah and her kittens up the back stairs to the nursery? My back has been turned what with a luncheon for guests to manage, so nothing is impossible. Nip up them steps and have a look-see. If she's not crooning to the kittens, I'd say she's still out and about.'

Lydia gripped an unpainted chair and sat down. 'If she's home, we'll hear her in good time. How are things in the parlour?'

Mrs Brummidge gave Lydia a look the girl could not read, waited a moment before continuing. 'You'd have to ask Rhoda. She's been doing the coming and going.'

Rhoda sat in the corner unthreading the runner beans. 'Lot of talky-talk in there, they had to open the windows to let the words out,' she said.

'How is the mighty Darwin? Is this part of a delayed victory lap?' The Great Oxford Debate several years ago, in which Darwin's theories had been attacked by Bishop Wilberforce (and defended by the family's distant cousin Thomas Huxley, among others), was by now old news but still fun. Even bootblacks, disagreeing about the proper practice of their trades, threatened to rent out the Oxford University Museum of Natural History to argue their positions. Still, those who regarded the Book of Genesis as factual took the notion of transmutation from beast to mankind very seriously indeed. Sedition, calumny, apostasy. There were some who said Darwin would be ill-advised to wander in dark Oxford lanes without a cosh and a pistol or, barring that, an agreeable gorilla to defend him against attacks from the spiritual thinkers of the day.

'I try not to overhear when I am retrieving the tray,' replied Rhoda, full of self-admiration, as if listening to Darwin hypothesize on pre-history might irritate her morals. 'He has added inches and fullness to his beard since his last visit. I'll say no more.'

'Perhaps he means to serve as a walking exhibit of Early Man before Tonsorial Parlours.' Lydia had her hands full with her own talents, appetites, delusions, and curiosities about life as it was lived in high June of 186_. Pre-history to a fifteen-year-old girl child means nothing further back in time than the courtship of her parents. 'I don't suppose Alice is in there with them? Rhoda?'

'No; just the master, and Darwin, and an associate visiting from Philadelphia or Boston, I believe, and his little black beetle.'

'Another specimen to examine? Is it pricked into a page with pins?'

'We don't gossip in my kitchen,' snorted Mrs Brummidge. Rhoda bent ostentatiously to her work. Lydia, included in the condemnation, felt chafed under instruction. She was imagining a campaign of insurrection, though had not settled on a strategy, when a knock sounded on the door from the passage.

'Goodness, could they not *ring* when they need attention?' hissed Mrs Brummidge. 'And me not done up proper to conduct a tour through the operations.' She adjusted her apron. She wiped some apple peels from where they'd clung to the cloth. She added, 'The master is bringing Darwin through to examine lower life-forms, Rhoda. Straighten your spine or you'll be mistook for a mollusc.'

'Maybe it's Alice's nurse, back early,' said Lydia.

'Miss Groader has gone to Banbury to deal with her ailing mother. She won't return until the morrow. That's why *you* were to be looking after Alice.' Arriving at the door to the passage, Mrs Brummidge opened it with a brusque gesture, part genuflection and part defensive crouch.

It was neither beardy Darwin nor the master, after all, but a younger gentleman in fine enough clothes to make both Rhoda and Lydia sit up. 'Ah, I've come to the right place,' he said. 'Always an exercise in temptations, which closed door to approach.' He spoke in one of the American accents; Lydia couldn't distinguish among them. To her they all sounded dry and tinny. Almost quack-like.

'What can I do for you, sir?' Mrs Brummidge was immune to the charms of a well-fitting waistcoat upon a trim male form if the form was a foreigner. The visitor had removed his jacket, as the parlour took the morning sun punishingly. In his shirt-sleeves and buttoned waistcoat he seemed the very grocer.

'I wondered if you might have some milk.'

Lydia stood and folded her hands together so the full impact of her juliette sleeves might register. 'I'm Lydia. The mistress of the house, more or less.'

'I beg your pardon.' He bowed and blushed. 'I'd been told you would not be at home today, and I assumed – how foolish of—' He all but swallowed his collar. 'Mr Winter, at your service.'

So now, an impasse. No further conversation was possible. Lydia despite her status in the household was no more than a hostage standing in the centre of this flour-strewn flagstone floor. This was Mrs Brummidge's domain.

The cook sniffed. 'We don't hold with milk drinking in this house unless there is a sick child. Too many vile particules. I could supply you with a glass of nut ale. Or a barley water. Take your choice. Unless the child is sick?'

'Child?' said Lydia. Affecting too maternal a tone would be a strain, and unconvincing; she tried merely for the investigative.

'Barley water would do nicely. Miss Lydia,' said Mr Winter, and bowed. 'Cook.' He glanced over at Rhoda and gave up, and disappeared.

'*Child?*' said Lydia, turning to Mrs Brummidge with lifted nostrils, suggesting outrage at not having been informed. But of course: hadn't Miss Armstrong mentioned another young scamp on the premises today?

'You do *such* a job keeping track of Alice,' retorted Mrs Brummidge. 'How mortifying, was you to lose a visiting child in the bargain. And one travelling with His Noxiousness Mr Darwin, no less.' (Mrs Brummidge did not care to imagine chimpanzees swinging from the branches of *her* family tree.)

'I'll take the lemon barley through when it is ready,' said Lydia.

'I wouldn't hear of it. A scandal. Rhoda, off your rump and look smart.' Though the *Mrs* was an honorific, Mrs Brummidge maintained a matron's sense of decorum. She enjoyed wielding it as a weapon. It was more effective than irony.

CHAPTER 14

Ada sat and leaned against the pedestal of the table. To judge by the solitary piece of furniture, she seemed to be in a hall for giants. Yet she could spy no entrance for them. The KEEP OUT door in the skirting board looked like one from a writing-desk cubby. Ada felt very small indeed. But agile, like a mouse, not like a broken toy lost under the settee. Surely she could worry her way through that door somehow? It seemed to be the only exit.

She scurried forwards and tried the knob again, in case it had changed its mind and wanted to open. It did not. But this time she thought to look through the keyhole.

What began as undifferentiated sheen organized itself into patches of green and blue. A lawn of some sort, a sky. A wall of topiary hedge clipped into the shapes of domesticated hens, as far as Ada could tell. Along came the Ace of Spades with the basket containing Rosa Rugosa, who was trailing her roots through the grass in a most unladylike display. Ada cupped her hands around the keyhole and called, 'Hallo, over here! Open the door!' But the Ace of Spades, if he even heard Ada, kept traipsing. His head was down, possibly to find a burying plot for Rosa.

Until now, Ada had been drifting through this unusual day with disregard for what she'd left behind and for what might lie ahead. Had it occurred to her to ask the question – *what is this adventure like?* – she might have concluded that her visit

seemed like a story or a dream. In any case, it didn't correspond
to life as she had known it so far.

A story in a book has its own intentions, even if unknowable
to the virgin reader, who just lollops along at her own pace
regardless of the author's strategies, and gets where she will.
After all, a book can be set aside for weeks, or for good. (Burned
in the grate.) Alternatively, a story can be adored for centuries.
But it cannot be derailed. A plot, whether abandoned by a reader
or pursued rapturously, remains itself, and gets where it is headed
even if nobody is looking. It is progressive and inevitable as the
seasons. Winter still comes after autumn though you may have
died over the summer.

As for dreams, they are powered by urgent desire, even if that
desire is only to escape the quotidian. Ada, who lived with a
sense of disappointment and failure, thanks to her misshapen
form, suffered from a flat dream-life, one that seemed poorly
differentiated from her waking hours. As a stolid child, her
dreams were of static things, almost still-lifes: a lump of cheddar
on a board, a goat roped to a tinker's cart, a curving road.

Now, however, Ada no longer felt like the passive observer
of an unfolding fiction or of a dream daguerreotype. Something
new rose in her, a thrill of ambition. She had to get into that
garden. She *would* get into that garden. She didn't know why
she felt so strongly about it. Usually she didn't much care for
gardens. The garden at the Vicarage was a mess, what with the
monkey-puzzle tree needing pruning and the orange hawkbit
colonizing the verge. But this garden looked entrancing, something like a college garden glimpsed through forbidding gates.
Such Oxford gardens would remain off-limits to the likes of
Ada, both for her gender and for her crab-gaited form. And
probably for her latent sinfulness. All the more important that
she gain access to this paradise in the keyhole.

She peered again. Beyond the door, the lawn was shorn and

rolled to Pythagorean precision. The clouds were perfect, neither too many nor histrionic. As she watched hungrily, the cumuli began sliding down the side of the world and changing places with the lawn. This proved disconcerting, like a picture in a book turned upside down. Why, there was the Ace of Spades digging a hole in the lawn-sky, and stuffing Rosa Rugosa root-first into the green-fringed heaven hovering over a blue eternal sky-sea. It was amusing to see the Ace of Spades sprinkle water upwards. 'This *is* a day I'm having,' said Ada to herself.

'No, it's not,' said a voice behind her. 'It's a day *I'm* having. You're only decoration. A sort of mousy, apprentice Erinys detached from her clot of spectres, I imagine. Lose your way?'

She turned and discovered a lopsided crescent moon hanging above and to one side of the glass tabletop. 'Did you speak?' she asked it. 'You, moon?'

The moon distorted itself to answer. 'You were expecting a Pantagruel come through for his cup of ocean? The instructions tell you: don't look up.'

'I was always taught to look a person in the eye when addressing them. Though it's difficult to do now. Your eyes are invisible.'

The moon-mouth said, 'I'm feeling hungry, but harpy or mouse, you are extremely odd-looking. I hope you don't taste untoward.'

'I am no mouse. I am a little girl.'

'You are either a *very* little girl or an indecisive Fate or an argumentative and dissembling mouse.' The sliver-moon began to seem more like a cat's mouth. Ada was glad the rest of the cat wasn't present, as a cat that size would scarcely leave room for her.

'Do you know how to get into the garden?' she asked, to change the subject.

'Through the door, of course. When it's ajar.'

A guttural hiss or a purr, Ada couldn't decide which, rumbled from behind the smiling moon-mouth. Then a tongue emerged from between pin-teeth. It angled to lick some invisible part of the implied cat. When Ada realized that the cat was probably bathing its particulars, she was glad the body was absent. Gigantic feline organs of any variety weren't included in the list of classic panoramas she might hope to glimpse before she died.

She thought it would be polite to divert attention from the practice of hygiene. 'The garden beyond that door is circling itself somehow.'

'No it isn't,' said the cat-mouth. 'It's the keyhole that's rotating.'

Ada looked again. Sure enough, the keyhole was moving in a clockwise direction, one complete rotation to the minute. 'I met a gardener who had a key. But he's already inside. Is there another key?' she asked.

'There may be, or may not be, but either way it means nothing to me. This is my day, after all, not yours. I have no interest in attending a garden party.'

'I should think we share the day equally,' ventured Ada.

'Impossible,' came the reply. 'I'm much larger than you are. So we can't share anything equally. Grow up a little and you'll see what I mean.'

'I would like to know what the tag on the teacup says. Since you are much more lofty than I, you could read it and tell me.'

One orange cat-eye appeared, and squinted at the tabletop. 'It says: DRINK ME.'

'I find that hard to believe.'

A bit more of the cat appeared, nearly its whole face, including a pair of twitching ears. A mask floating against walnut wainscoting. 'I could carry you in my mouth and deposit you on the tabletop if you like, and you could see for yourself if I'm lying.' The smile now looked like a leer.

Ada was afraid if she walked into the cat's mouth she might fall out the other side. What would Miss Armstrong say? 'I'd better not,' she said. 'I know a little bit about the damned crowding into Charon's boat, but I don't know much about ghosts, including ghost cats. There might be some contagion, and I don't think I'm ready to be a ghost.'

'No time like the present. Can't I interest you in a little bite?' The mouth loomed. 'I think you are wearing a tag that says EAT ME, but you have hidden it in your clothes. That's why mice shouldn't wear clothes.'

Ada said, 'I have only one life. I need to take care of it.'

'Very well said. Off and away with the fairies, indeed. *That* was a smart move.' Ada couldn't tell if the spectral cat was mocking her. It continued. 'They buried *me* under the Iffley yew. A new grave was open and they packed me on top of a coffin before they filled in the hole. It's true cats have nine lives, you know. But cats can't count. So I don't know where I am.'

'I don't know where I am either. But I know where I want to be. Won't you please tell me where I can find another key?'

The cat-head didn't reply, but set to licking the ocean out of the teacup. As it beaded up on the cat's whiskers, it no longer looked like drops of salty sea, but like cream. 'Since this is *my* day, by and large, I have no reason to satisfy the urges of the most peculiar mouse I have ever met. Still, I'm feeling fat and satisfied. *Do* climb into my mouth, my dear. More than one way to get into that garden, you know.'

At great speed, the mouth dipped very close to her. The smile looked less hungry than kind, but Ada stepped back. 'I am too timid,' she said, 'and we've hardly been introduced. Another time, perhaps.'

The haunted mouth began to fade. 'Very well. I can wait. May I give you a bit of advice?'

'Please do.'

'Don't take the advice of anyone you meet here. We're all mad.'

Ada thought about it. I've just met *you,* and your advice is not to trust you. If I *don't* take your advice, then I *should* trust you. I guess I have to trust you and not trust you. Your advice wheels about like the keyhole. There's no way in.

Watching the cat-head dissolve much as daylight does, by unnamable degrees, Ada's eyes fell again on the words in the ceiling tracery. DON'T LOOK UP. Why trust *that* advice? Noticing that the plaster tracery had sent tendrils down the panelling, and that they were beginning to take root in the floor, she found a foothold and then a second. She began to climb towards the green heaven.

CHAPTER 15

Mrs Brummidge poured; Mrs Brummidge squeezed the lemons; Mrs Brummidge scooped the sugar; Mrs Brummidge took a great wooden spoon and stirred the concoction. 'Whilst you was out reading and losing track of Alice,' she said to Lydia, 'that governess from the Vicarage came sniffing about for Ada Boyce, who'd been sent here with a jar of marmalade. But we never seen her, nor the marmalade, which will be welcome should it ever arrive.'

'Young ladies these days,' said Lydia, deciding how to proceed. 'One would think there were gypsies about, the way small girls disappear.'

'Well, our Alice has her own compass, no doubt about that and don't we know it well. But Ada Boyce is docile as a lambkin.'

'A mammoth, compromised lambkin.'

'Don't be snidey. Ada's taking off on her lonesome vexes her governess no end. You've not seen the poor afflicted child, did you?'

'Well, I did. And then I did not,' said Lydia. 'I said as much to Miss Armstrong as she flurried by me after having accosted you for news. She's a high-spirited ostrich, not made for patience, I think.'

'Well, that *household*,' said Mrs Brummidge darkly.

'What do you mean?'

'I once went by to borrow some malt vinegar. That time the

grocer was gone away. Due to his old gaffer's getting his head split open by a falling chamber pot. The kitchen door of the Vicarage was open to the sun and their cook didn't hear my knock, so I stepped inside.' Mrs Brummidge looked this way and that, as if there were agents who might hear her spilling testimony against the House of Boyce. 'She was drinking *tea* from the *spout*. Oh, it's an ill-run house, from garret to cistern. I don't wonder Miss Armstrong flusters so.' At this she caught herself. Too much had been said. She finished up with the lemon barley. She whisked a tray from the shelves beneath the window. 'Rhoda, look smart. They'll be waiting for this.'

Lydia stood. 'Rhoda, keep at your beans.' The kitchen maid was flummoxed, as if caught between a constable and a clergyman and unsure whom to obey. At Lydia's insurrection Mrs Brummidge took a sluice of air between her teeth and backward-whistled it in. But she said no more about it. She placed the tray with the lemon barley and some drinking glasses and a plate of morning cake upon the pastry table. She retreated, as if the refreshments were about to detonate. She trained her eyes on the floor. Rhoda settled her rump back on her three-legged stool.

Lydia didn't speak again, but picked up the tray. She led with her shoulder through the swinging door into the passage. When she was halfway along, she heard Mrs Brummidge hiss at Rhoda, 'Unseemly!' with the same tone of scandal she might have used had she been saying 'Strumpet!' or 'Baptist!' She does have her opinions, does our Mrs Brummidge, thought Lydia. She was stymied for a moment at the parlour door, which was closed. How does one knock and open a door while carrying a tray? How did Rhoda ever manage? Balancing one edge of the tray against her bosom, Lydia freed her right hand to knock. Then she went through, into the male preserve of Pater, Mr Darwin, and that handsome Mr Winter.

The light was bright. The breeze off the Cherwell delivered

an odour of June mud, backwashed with essence of meadow-grass and a whiff of cow. Mr Winter was quiet and attentive, lifting on his toes before the open window. His hands were clasped in downward prayer. His eyes did not tilt towards the door. Nor did those of Pater or of Darwin. But Lydia could hardly blame them. They were expecting no one more exotic than Rhoda.

She set the tray down on top of the closed harmonium. Her back turned to them, Lydia listened intently to the men. Darwin seemed to be reading from his own manuscript, line by line. Pater was commenting in words of solemn circumspection. It reminded Lydia of the way the local boys would beat the bounds of the parish every year, with peeled willow wands and high hilarity. Of hilarity there was none from Darwin, nor from dear Father, but the intensity of thrashing seemed to her the same. Every yard of statement needed to be tested for soundness. What Mr Winter was adding, other than devotion to the holy cause of thought, was unclear.

Lydia rotated at the hip, waiting for a pause in the proceedings so she could offer to serve. Mr Winter against the bright window was a silhouette. His hair was silvery blond and sleek. His form was neater even than it had seemed in the kitchen. How nice that he wasn't lost in one of those sexless black gowns in which the scholars tramped about, hooting in sunshine and huddling in rain.

A patch of shadow in a darker corner of the room shifted from beside the aureole afforded Mr Winter. Lydia started, making a small, contained movement. Was Alice hiding in here all along? Impossible. But the shape was childlike. 'Mercy upon us,' she said with displeasure. Darwin paid no mind. Pater looked up. She could not turn towards Mr Winter.

'Lydia, whatever are you doing?' said her father.

'I am here to deliver a beverage, Pater, as requested by your other guest. I had been told there was a child. I see I had not been told everything.'

The creature came forward. His countenance was of a very un-English hue. He was of Africa, or from some plantation in Hispaniola or Barbados or the like. His skin was shiny as oiled mahogany. Hair cropped as if for nits. With undisguised thirst, he cast his glance upon the drink. 'Yes, this is meant for you,' she said. His hands came out to clasp the glass before she had filled it. For an instant she saw his hands were gammon-pink upon the palms. This surprised her, as the boy was otherwise as coal-dusty as a sweep at the end of his fourth flue of the day.

Darwin went back to his text, her father to his exegetic murmuring. Mr Winter moved across the carpet so he could speak in a lowered tone. 'Miss Lydia, you honour us,' he said.

'No one mentioned the child was a boy,' she replied, in tones even lower, 'and an aboriginal at that.'

'May I present him to you? Miss Lydia, this is Siam.' The boy didn't meet her eyes. He downed the lemon drink like a Berber lately crawled from hot Sahara sands.

'What is he doing here? With – with them? With you?' She realized it might sound uncouth, her enquiry, but she could be considered the mistress of the house, by some accountings anyway. She threw back her shoulders to suggest authority.

'Well, miss, the lad's travelling with me, you see. I'd arrived at Down House to meet the great man. I'd a letter of introduction. To my surprise, despite his recent aversion to travel, Darwin announced he'd made a previous appointment to visit your father' – at this Mr Winter's voice became a whisper – 'in his bereavement. My unexpected arrival was timely. I was invited to come along and assist, as Darwin is too frail to travel alone.'

'Yes,' said Lydia, also in private tones, 'but – but. This boy. He seems young to be your servant.'

'No, no; not a servant, you're right about that,' said Mr Winter hastily, as if that explained everything.

'Mother has been dead for several months. Why has Darwin come now? And why have you bothered to come with him?' Lydia felt she was asking questions too grand for the custom of the parlour; she might well continue with, *And why did Mother die, and where did she go?* But she stood looking at Mr Winter with a ferocity that, though she had no idea of it, was nearly glamorous.

'I understand that your father was kind to Huxley when he was here defending Darwin's theories against the charges of heresy. Darwin has his head in natural science, but everyone has lost someone,' explained the guest, hushedly. 'Darwin his daughter Annie, this house its beloved matriarch. The heart is a construct of any waking creature, and Darwin has a heart, too.'

'A heart *and* a mind. I suppose Pater wants to discuss the immortal soul with Mr Darwin.' She sighed, as if it was a recurrent argument about interior plumbing.

'The great man is not well,' said Mr Winter. 'He lives in his sickroom. Had I not shown up opportunely upon his doorstep, he'd never have managed this trip. I can see it is taking a toll. I should go back to his side.'

The little boy had finished a second glass. 'There will be none for the others,' said Lydia rudely. 'Though I suppose I can negotiate a fresh supply. How does this scamp come to be with you?'

'He can speak for himself. He speaks English quite well. Perhaps you would like to show him around, now he is comfortable here? He's slightly bored.'

The world of men, always reconvening, asserting itself. The pull of her father's susurrus, Darwin's cautious replies. Mr Winter preferred that over conversation with her. 'Very well,' she said. 'Master Siam, is it? You may accompany me. You may tell me something about yourself.'

The lad followed her willingly enough, only pausing at the

door to glance bright-eyed at his guardian. Mr Winter had returned to the window. He'd struck up again the posture of acolyte. An Athenian harkening to Socrates. 'Come along lest you get lost, too,' said Lydia to the child.

CHAPTER 16

Ada hadn't climbed more than a few yards up the strut-work of the great hall before she saw that the flanking curlicues of plaster were no longer symmetrical. Now they seemed to be teased into variety. The cold moulded surface fragmented in her hands as she climbed. It crumbled like old moss, revealing the suppleness of living wood. She turned to look about her. She realized that the hall had turned back into a forest. She was climbing one of dozens of trees growing so closely together that she could see no horizon.

What about the teacup, the tag, she thought. She looked down. Perhaps she could read it from above? But she'd achieved too great a height already. The table below her had lengthened, and covered itself with a cloth, upon which several dozen teacups and quite a few pots of tea were set about in a higglety-pigglety fashion. She couldn't identify the original teacup among them from this vantage. Well, when I finish seeing where I am, she thought, I shall climb back down and have a spot of tea.

It felt wonderful to climb. Her feet possessed a new and certain stepping-knowledge that they had never had on paving stones or staircases. At home, the very pattern in the carpet could trip her up, it seemed.

Ada wasn't the type to analyse her moods, generally. Even now she didn't dwell on the idea of elation. But she felt it as she climbed. A promised view often lifts the heart.

She was reaching a point where the canopy was becoming thinner. She had to be careful to settle her foot squarely in each forking branch for fear of cracking it and tumbling earthwards. The light intensified. The sky, a peerless blue, seemed very much a shire and not a London sky, she observed. She hoped she might somehow see into the garden where the Ace of Spades had been busy planting Rosa Rugosa.

'I imagine you have the right papers for this neck of the woods?' asked a voice curtly.

Ada craned. 'I never thought of the neck of the woods as being near the top of the trees, but I suppose it makes sense.'

'You're approaching the crown of the tree, so of course you're at the neck of the woods,' snapped the voice. Its owner fluttered near. 'We've had a serpent scare recently. We can't be too careful. We've hired an agent to ensure security. I imagine he grilled you right proper before allowing you access.'

'That cat with the floating smile?'

'Cat! Mind your tongue! Cat indeed! As if!' The bird shook her wings like a creature emerging from a birdbath. 'While serpents are a menace to eggs in the nest, cats are notorious for slaying birds. No, I'm talking about the Head Egg below, the one who cleared your travel papers.'

'I have no papers, and no one cleared them.'

'Perhaps he saw them and cleared them away, and that's why you haven't got them any more,' said the bird. 'If you haven't got any papers, though, do you actually recall who you are and what you are doing here?'

'If you please, my name is Ada.'

'Adder! I knew it! And a very fat adder at that. You shall find no mercy from *me*!' At this the little bird began to fly in Ada's face, beating and shrieking.

'I'm not an adder, please! I'm a girl.'

The bird returned to a branch and cocked her head to look

with one eye, then twisted about to look with a second. '*Another* girl? I'm not sure I believe you. The serpent said she was a girl, too, but I never saw a girl with such a long neck. I imagine she thought *she* was being the neck of the woods. She was only drawing attention to herself in an unseemly fashion, if you ask me.'

Ada had almost forgotten about Alice. '*Have* you seen another girl? Was she called Alice, by any chance?'

'If I knew I wouldn't say. You are all in cahoots, a league of serpents. Go away or I'll call the Head Egg.'

Ada was about to suggest that the bird do just that, as Ada rather liked the notion of a large egg in charge of domestic tranquillity. She wanted to see how such a campaign might be carried out. However, just then she heard the noise, not too far off, of breaking branches. A disorganized mechanical ruckus, more or less at the same height as Ada and her interlocutor, though out of sight behind screens of foliage.

'There it is again, that infernal groaning and thwacking. Something has been worrying itself into conniptions over that way. I would go to look but I daresn't leave my nest, not with serpents about.'

'You *can* trust me. I'm no serpent, I'm a girl.'

'A serpent can change its skin, you know, and appear to us in all manner of guises.' This sounded like something the Reverend Boyce would declare. Before Ada could ask herself whether perhaps she *was* a kind of serpent without knowing it, the bird continued. 'Whatever it is over there, I hope it comes and catches you. It ratchets, it creaks, it breaks branches. The Bandersnatch, for all I know. Frumiouser and frumiouser, by the sound of it. I wish it would go away. Would you care to be engaged as a Bandersnatch-snatcher?'

'No, thank you.' Ada shuddered. A storm of tattered leaves rose in the air a short distance away, suggesting proximity of danger. 'I may have to do without the view that I'd climbed all the way up here to see. Perhaps I should have minded the instructions. The ceiling did advise me not to look up.'

'That was my doing,' said the bird. 'I thought I would advertise against craning and preening, so as to prevent serpents from noticing the eggs in my nest. A new mother would kill to protect her young, you know.' Her feathers drooped. 'Of course my strategy didn't keep you out.'

'I've been advised not to take advice,' said Ada, to soothe her.

The bird replied promptly, 'Then may *I* advise that you stay and join me in the rearing of my latest clutch of eggs.'

'No, thank you,' said Ada. 'I'm afraid of the Bandersnatch, or whatever it is. And I may be late for tea.' She could no longer see the table laid out beneath the limbs of the trees, but she hoped it was still there, and that the tea was still hot.

'It's acceptable to be late for tea in this neck of the woods,' said the bird. 'Indeed, it's inevitable, as we never serve tea here. Did you mention you were leaving? If you see the Head Egg, tell him he has fallen down on the job.'

'Oh, I hope he hasn't,' said Ada, beginning to reverse her footsteps. 'When an egg falls, well, it can't easily be repaired, even with Mrs Winslow's Soothing Syrup. "All the king's horses and all the king's men couldn't put Humpty together again."'

'You *are* a serpent, always on about fallen eggs,' said the bird. 'We birds live above reproach.'

'I hope I am not descending to meet reproach,' said Ada, being clever.

'All who descend meet reproach,' said the bird, with fine moral feeling.

CHAPTER 17

The boy followed Lydia down the steps to the kitchens. She had no interest in exposing him to the gawps of Rhoda or Mrs Brummidge, but what else was she to do with him?

'More to drink, more cake,' Lydia announced as she came through, like a regular domestic. 'I left the jug and the other glasses behind, but this little prince is ravenous.'

'Poor tyke,' said Mrs Brummidge, bustling. Rhoda jumped with a start. She looked as if she'd been reading up on cholera in London and the filthy well at Broad Street, and she'd become a convert to Snow's theory of germ contagion. She inched away from the boy as if she might catch something wretched from him.

The kitchen door stood open to cucumber frames and a few ill-trimmed old fruit trees whose heavy arthritic limbs were supported with crutches. The light that slanted in, the taint of meadowsweet upon the aqueous breeze, the sound of doves now at their elevenses, these all conferred upon Siam an air of normalcy. He looked like a boy who might need Dinah the cat, or her kittens, to play with. For a moment Lydia hated him for his ordinariness. There ought to be a credit of the exotic about him, but his eyes looked just like a boy's eyes, no different.

She was tired of playing mother after just a few moments. She was after all hardly fifteen. Finding this novelty of humanity upon her threshold, what *would* Mama have done?

But questions of that sort could have no answer. The subjunctive mood was not Logic Lane. It was no detour, only a cul-de-sac. Answers to the question *what Mama would have done*: they did not exist, for one could never know. Had Mrs Clowd not died at the end of Michaelmas term, her husband wouldn't have received a belated visit of condolence from the great Darwin. Some gibbering American named Winter wouldn't have come up from London to hold Darwin's elbow at every step. This ebony boy would be scratching the backs of his knees in some other room than this.

'I don't suppose you have a name,' said Mrs Brummidge offhandedly to the boy.

'Do too.'

'So do I, it's Mrs Brummidge.' As if she talked to specimen children every day of the week, as natural as that. She lumbered about, cutting an extra large slice of cake for him. 'Now you tell me your moniker, and we'll be done with this little bit of business.'

'Siam,' he said. 'Siam Winter. Winter,' he repeated.

Lydia couldn't bring herself to ask how he came by Mr Winter's name. 'Shall I get Dinah from upstairs? She's probably dozing on Alice's window-seat, or on Nurse Groader's coverlet.'

'I'll go,' said Rhoda, and fled.

'Are you visiting in England or have you come to live?' asked Mrs Brummidge.

Siam shrugged. His neck was bony but his chin lovely and stunted. When he glanced around, Lydia slid an extended peek. She hadn't imagined such ruddiness possible in a boy of his origins. He caught her looking. He pursed his lips, as if trying to keep his tongue from sticking itself out at her.

'Not Egyptian, I'd guess, nor Italian,' said Mrs Brummidge. 'Would you be from the sugar islands then?'

'Siam is in the Far East, Mrs Brummidge,' said Lydia.

'No, I ain't,' said the boy.

'Where – do – you – come – from?' asked Lydia, as if addressing the deaf.

'The parlour,' he said, crooking a thumb over his shoulder.

Stifling a smile, Mrs Brummidge commenced to dicing the rhubarb for her syllabub. 'Either very quick or very slow, that one,' she commented, 'but luncheon wants to be ready when they ring for it. Why don't you take the boy for a stroll, Lydia? Whilst you're about it, you *will keep an eye out for Alice*. Do you hear me? Her father will notice her absence sooner or later, and you'll answer to him if anything happens to her.' A clucking of tongues, a soft shaking of the head at the sorrows of incompetent parenting.

It wasn't that Lydia objected to being seen with a child of equatorial origins. It was that she wouldn't know what to say should anyone meet her in the lane down to the meadows. While Lydia didn't think she was insensitive to the plight of others – the colour of his skin, his curious rubicund health! – she was careful of her own profile in the community. Anyone might note her discomfiture and take it to be for the wrong reason. 'Alice would be some help right now,' complained Lydia. Alice wouldn't bother with Siam's race; she wouldn't notice it. Just as she had never commented on Ada's bracing armature.

Mrs Brummidge *would* go on and on about a thing. 'Miss Alice was in your charge. It's fine for her to be larking about all lonesome, but she's too young to be gone for too long.'

'I dozed and she dawdled off,' said Lydia. 'She'll dawdle back, as usual. She doesn't go near the water, and everyone knows her, so there's no need to fret.'

'I worry for Miss Alice, I worry for her father. We're taking care of him now, mind.' But before Mrs Brummidge could work up to a fine hectoring, Rhoda came back with Dinah's two kittens, the black and the white.

They brought Siam up from his somnolent caution, those kittens. They capered and tottered and mewed with great fantastic faces on their frail necks. He fell on his knees to adore them. They pounced upon his thighs and bounced away again, as if everything they touched were shot through with static, the sort promised by dry air and thready cotton blankets. 'They's a pair of little demons,' he cried. Scrapping like Lucifer and Michael, the black and the white, over and over so fast they might almost have been two grey kittens.

They paused, suddenly mature, studying. The black one deigned to lick its uneven fur. Siam took something out of his jacket pocket to dangle and attract its twin. His back was turned to the room, and Lydia couldn't make out what he had – a toy of some sort, a worsted ball perhaps, or a scrap of rasher filched from some breakfast platter? Then a knock on the door sounded. In came Mr Winter, less tentatively this time.

'They've begun to talk on personal matters,' he said, 'and it seemed proper for me to leave them in peace. I shall take a constitutional. Siam, come. It'll do you good to stretch your legs after your long morning.'

'I'll come, too,' said Lydia. Mrs Brummidge shot her quite the look. 'You *suggested* I take the boy out, and that I collect Alice,' she continued, 'so I'll escort Mr Winter around the path towards Parks Road and the great case of reptilian bones. Have you yet seen the University Museum, Mr Winter?'

Mrs Brummidge couldn't contain herself. 'But Miss Lydia! Walking about with a gentleman you've just met? Not without your father's say, and I'll march in there and—'

'Oh, he can't be disturbed. He is indisposed,' said Mr Winter. He made a gesture, a finger at the lips, a *shhhh*. It was unseemly for being intimate.

'You'll need a chaperone then at the very least. Rhoda, off your posterior, and no jaw.'

'We have a chaperon,' said Lydia sweetly. 'Little Siam, don't you know.'

She stood and pressed down the front of her skirt. Was it too warm to require a shawl? In any case, a bonnet would be proper. She would get one presently. For the moment, she stood bare-headed, willing a stiff sudden breeze to come in off the water and meadow and stir her hair just so. And you might have guessed her a minor goddess, for all that, because the breeze did as she imagined it might. Her hair blew fetchingly about her pale cheeks and severe expression.

CHAPTER 18

Ada had climbed down to where there were no more branches. She could see the green grass below. It looked generous and soft, like feather blankets. Previously, in the world above worlds (DON'T LOOK UP), had she been able to scale a tree in the first place, she'd have been paralysed on the descent. She'd have had to summon a gardener with a ladder to rescue her. Had she jumped, her legs would have been too rigid to provide coil and spring upon landing. They'd have absorbed the impact like ivory jackstraws, and shattered.

Ada was, however, not above-world, and so she jumped down.

She landed without disaster. Indeed, it was almost fun. No, it *was* quite fun, pleasurable. She had half a mind to climb back up and do it again, but the other half of her mind was ready for a refreshment. The tea was laid out for a party of several dozen, as far as she could tell. She brushed herself off to make herself presentable. She pushed through ferny underbrush to approach the table set out *en plein air*.

More than one table pushed together, it seemed. At various places they jutted out, at one point making a T. Unmatching chairs were arrayed, some helter-skelter, pushed back as if guests had fled in haste. Elsewhere, chairs were neatly aligned in sequence, awaiting company. At the far end, at a particularly dingy patch of tablecloth, a couple of characters were nattering away. They froze when they heard her approach.

'Don't look now,' said a small, intense man in a top hat, 'but I believe we have a burglar.'

'When may I look?' replied his companion, who had promptly clasped paws over its eyes. It was a Hare of some variety, naked of ornament but for a key on a chain around its neck.

'I'm not a burglar,' said Ada.

'Clever alibi,' said the man, chomping on a bit of bread. 'Many would believe you. I, for one, am not fooled.'

'Ooh,' said the Hare, peeking. 'She *is* beautiful. She has stolen my heart.'

'I rest my case,' said the Hatter, for that's what he seemed to be, now that Ada could see a card reading *10/6* jauntily stuck in the silken hatband that announced the price as ten shillings and sixpence. 'Have some tea, but don't steal the spoons.'

'I would welcome some tea, but I would never steal a spoon,' said Ada.

'So you're a liar now, too. What's that you've got in your pocket?'

'How do you know I have anything in my pocket?' asked Ada.

'I can see the handle sticking out.'

Ada felt in her pinafore. She withdrew a spoon. 'Oh, this. Yes, well they were dosing the baby with some corrective. I cadged a portion. I put this in my pocket to bring downstairs, but I forgot. I promise that it doesn't belong to you.'

'It doesn't *now*,' said the Hare. 'I'd recognize that pattern anywhere, though.'

Ada laid it on the table next to the nearest spoon. 'They're as near twins as spoons can be,' said the Hatter.

'They're nothing at all alike,' said Ada.

'Not all twins are identical,' said the Hatter. 'I have a twin called Hatta, and *he* has a twin called Hatter. You can imagine the confusion when we all try to reserve a table at one of the finer establishments.' He looked about dolefully.

'*Are* there any establishments around here?' asked Ada.

'They wouldn't dare,' said the Hatter. 'How do you find the tea?'

'It's quite – well, it seems quite salty, I'm afraid.'

'It's an awful curse to be frightened of salt. You must jump at your own tears.'

'It's all a matter of taste, I expect,' replied Ada. 'How do *you* find it?'

'Why, I look down in my cup, and there it is. If it were a bear it would bite me.'

At this the lid of a teapot fell off. A Dormouse poked its nose up. Its whiskers twitched. It said drowsily, 'Is she gone?'

'She's right here,' said the Hare, waving a spoon of its own towards Ada.

The Dormouse craned its thick furry neck. 'That's not Alice. That's a different one.'

'Must be her twin,' said the Hare. 'Don't touch the brioches, darling, we're saving them for the Duchess, if she ever arrives.'

'You've seen Alice,' said Ada. 'She's been here!'

'She marched through a little while ago,' said the Hare. 'How long ago was that, Hatter?'

'Not as long as all that,' said the little man, munching on toast.

'Were you already in the middle of your tea?' asked Ada.

'We don't know, do we,' said the Hatter. 'Until we're done, we don't know when the middle might be. We may be just beginning. Eternity is gruelling – not that we're serving gruel, mind. But this tea party may go on for hundreds of years. Right now, I couldn't possibly say.'

'I could,' said the Dormouse. 'But I won't.' It clamped the lid on top of its head like a little beanie and sank into the teapot. However its friends cajoled, it would not come out again. It whistled a popular melody through the teapot-spout, though, which unsettled Ada. It sounded ghostly.

'I had forgotten that I was looking for Alice,' she said. 'Which way did she go, do you know?'

'She went forwards,' said the Hare decisively, 'for no one has yet found a way to go back.' He began to sing to the tune of the Dormouse.

> *'Though many would reclaim their youth,*
> *They soon must learn the dreaded truth*
> *That even should they homeward stray*
> *They'd find their youth had been stolen away.'*

'If their youth had been stolen and they found it, they'd have it again,' said Ada.

'Cleverness becomes a thief. I suspect she's up to mischief.' The Hatter pointed his spoon at Ada and turned to the Hare. 'I'd keep my thumb upon the *Kuchen, mein* Hare. Remember what happened to the tarts. A messy business, that. We haven't seen the end of it yet. Child, why are you looking for Alice?'

'Because she is lost,' said Ada.

'She did not look lost to me,' said the Hare. 'All the while she was here, she was as solid a little janissary as you'd care to see. Every time I looked over at her, there she was. With that alarming forehead. You could hardly miss her. It was like having Gibraltar to tea.'

'Did she say where she was going?' asked Ada. 'She has a tendency to wander about, you see. Someone will be worrying about her.'

'No doubt,' said the Hare. 'I can't say I noticed where she went, Hatter, did you? We were deep in conversation when she left.'

'We were talking about where she might go if she ever got up from the chair,' said the Hatter. 'Then, we looked up, she was gone. So we never found out.'.

Ada felt a twinge of impatience. 'This is important. If I could just steal a moment of your time and ask you, please, to try to remember—'

'Stealing again. And time is all we have, really,' said the Hare sadly.

'Time for tea,' declared the Hatter. 'The Madeira cake beckons. Shall we?'

They moved a few places to the right, where new cups were set cleanly upon unmatching saucers. Further along the table, the ornamental cake stand got up. It humped itself a few places away and squatted again.

'All this talk about stealing,' said Ada. 'Have *you* stolen her?'

'I stole a glance at her,' admitted the Hare. 'So shoot me.'

'She was an honest soul,' said the Hatter, 'if a bit dim.'

'That's not a very nice thing to say.'

'No, it isn't,' he agreed. 'Nor is it very tufted, or chartreuse, or miasmic, or palindromic. It's actually quite a dim thing to say, but that's what she was. Dim.'

'You are making me quite cross,' said Ada. 'I'm leaving.'

'She's trying to steal away,' whistled the Dormouse through the spout.

'She'd take anything that isn't nailed down. The damson *gâteau* is at grave risk of abduction. After her,' said the Hatter, pouring a new cup of tea.

'After *you*,' said the Hare politely.

'After all is said and done,' said the Dormouse, 'there is nothing to be done. Or said.' It fell silent, a little wistfully.

The Hatter lifted his cup and examined the dregs intently. The Hare took advantage of its companion's abstraction to spring from its chair. In a few bounds it had caught up with Ada. It pulled the chain from around its neck and put it around Ada's. 'Here,' said the Hare. 'I shall give you this in exchange for the spoon you left behind. I wouldn't like anyone to think I had stolen it. The Queen maintains the stiffest penalty for stealing. The death sentence. You will find this key uncommonly poor for measuring out treacle, but perhaps you can learn to do without treacle. Many do.'

Before Ada could thank the Hare, she heard a loud crashing in the woods behind her, as if a piece of the Hythe Bridge had fallen out of the trees. An iron sound, dangerous. She didn't ask the Hare where Alice might have been heading, but ran in the opposite direction of the crash. When she looked back, the Hare had returned to the table and was tying the edge of the tablecloth around its neck like a sort of bib. The Hatter was weeping bitterly. Ada thought she heard him say, 'She has stolen the *Stollen*.' She didn't pause to object, but pressed on through the forest, which was growing darker.

CHAPTER 19

Out of doors they assembled, a most uncommon grouping in Lydia's experience. This child in his easy loping amble, his splendid coffee-bean skin not exactly a novelty in these lanes, but not so common as to go unnoticed.

This boy, this Siam; and Lydia, in her own weeds of mourning. How well her fair hair showed as it spilled upon the dark shoulders of her summer shawl.

And then this American reed, quicksilver and grave at once, this Mr Winter. He must have a Christian name, though Lydia had no idea if it might be proper to ask about it outright. With the death of Lydia's mother had come, alas, the loss of maternal guidance. Mrs Brummidge groused and grumbled, of course; a cook doesn't count. Old Nurse Groader had opinions, and shared them. Still, a nurse can be relied upon to be old-fashioned, raised up, as such termagants always are, to promote the mores of a hundred years past.

Other nearby female influences? Disconcertingly few. The wives of some neighbours, who found Alice less winsome than weird, and treated Lydia like a Cerberus, skirting her as they approached the Croft with platters of cold sliced roast something or buckets of summer pudding, meant to console and attract the poor widower. Also an elderly spinster cousin in Cumnor, whose dislike for Lydia was returned in spades. Of other relatives there remained none except Lydia's maternal grandmother. Upon the death of her only child, though, the old lady had been struck with an affliction binding her tongue to silence. For her own good care she'd been removed to a sanatorium up the Banbury Road. If she had opinions about Lydia's deportment, ailment required the scold to keep her thoughts to herself.

And so I'm on my own, Lydia thought, as they passed through the gate and into the lane towards the river meadows and, eventually, the University Parks and the Oxford University Museum of Natural History. If conversation lagged she could take Mr Winter and young Siam through and show them the claw of the dodo, so sensibly extinct.

In silence she began to assemble what she knew of the Museum. It wasn't much. The construction had been funded by the sale of Bibles, a strategy intended to console those who found the close study of nature unseemly if not heretical. Nature is the second book of God, she reminded herself, preparing a defence in case Mr Winter was religious to a fault, like so many Americans as she'd heard it told. Or was God the second book of Nature? She couldn't remember. Perhaps she'd better avoid the Museum altogether. They'd keep to the riverbank.

She needn't have worried. Once free of the scholastic silence of the old Croft, Mr Winter became expansive. His heels scuffed at the gravelly track with such force that stones skipped about. He talked of the excitement of being in London for the first time, so far from home, so warmly welcomed thanks to the letters of introduction he had carried.

'But where is your home, when you are at home,' Lydia asked, and even more bravely, 'where is his?' Siam was skipping ahead down the path, eager as a beagle to see what lay around the next turn.

'Here, and thereabouts, and wherever,' said Mr Winter. 'We move as we might. Those in allegiance to abolition show boundless courtesy.'

'I'd thought that slavery matter settled, what with your proc-lamations and amendments and such. I mean, I know about your war, but isn't your Lincoln the local Lord Mansfield?' Lydia hoped they wouldn't become bogged down in a discussion of the times. The only current affair that mattered was the death of her mother. 'Our nation gave up the slave trade forty years ago, when Bishop Wilberforce's father made a forceful case against it.'

'The law says one thing, and custom another,' replied Mr Winter. 'What the assemblies legislate and what happens on the back roads of small towns are not always in agreement. Put another way, history takes a long time to happen.'

'I have always lived *here*,' said Lydia, trying to draw him back to the subject. 'When you go home, where will you go?'

But he appeared not to hear her. 'Will you stay on in Oxford, now that your mother has passed on?'

She felt impatient. 'Of course. We are not tinkers in caravans. And my father has his work.'

'What work is that, besides support to the defenders of Darwinism?'

'Pater crawls back and forth in underground corridors, retrieving books requested by scholars in the Bodleian.' She didn't want to talk about her father. 'Have you a Christian name, Mr Winter, or are you so deeply Darwinist that you have become a pagan?'

'You shock me, as you intend.' His tone was mocking.

She considered behaving as if chastised. She dropped her eyes to her hands, which were clasped at her waist. He took mercy, though. He said, 'Yes, I am Josiah Winter. I do not know if local practice permits you to call me Josiah, but I would permit it, if I may address you as Lydia.'

'Americans take liberties,' she acknowledged. 'Josiah.'

How far down the primrose path will I stray today? she wondered.

'He is in my care, is Siam,' said Josiah Winter. 'He has been so, Lydia, ever since a member of our New England congregation received a package containing the severed ear of a recovered slave.'

'I don't understand.' She hoped he would recognize in her voice a request for restraint. He carried on, as Americans will, deaf to certain subtleties.

'Have you heard of the Underground Railroad?' he asked her.

'I presume you are not talking about those tunnels being dug about Paddington and such.' She was trying to be light-hearted.

'Siam and some of his kin were headed for Canada West, where slavery has been outlawed several decades now,' he said. 'But bounty hunters caught up with them. Siam alone escaped. He has been under my protection since. He is likely to remain with me until his liberty can be promised by civil law. And so I've brought him abroad, for his own safety.'

'He has taken your name,' she said.

'I have given it to him.' A mild correction, saying much she could not interpret.

It was nearly as far as she felt prepared to go on the matter. Siam Winter was leaping about, laughing at bovinity. 'I cannot imagine his ordeals, but he has survived them well,' she said. 'I assume Mrs Winter has skills in the kitchen, or she has engaged a cook who knows what boys require to thrive.'

'Oh, there is no Mrs Winter,' replied Mr Winter.

CHAPTER 20

Ada stopped a short way into the forest. She could no longer hear the Hatter and the Hare. The light was low, but it was a green gloaming rather than a dusky one. The woods grew dense. Huge clusters of flowers of a pale soapsuds colour, almost lavender grey, drooped from aged vines. 'They are something like wisteria,' she found herself saying aloud, 'and something not.'

'A gentleman out strolling in the meadow!' cried an eager voice. 'Just what I hoped to see.'

It took Ada a few moments to locate the source of that remark. An elderly man in a rusty coat of chain mail was rooted to the earth by thick ropes of vine. They had grown up around him, coiling woody tendrils around his legs and waist and arms. Even as Ada watched, new fingerlets of green stretched to explore his ears and the wispy white hair upon his pate.

'I'm hardly a gentleman,' she replied, 'and this is hardly a meadow.'

'And I am hardly surprised,' he replied. 'I tend to muddle. Dear sir, would you be so kind as to untwist this vine from me? I fear I shall be late for the occasion.'

Ada went to work with a will. She tugged at the newest shoots because they were most supple. When they snapped, she began struggling with the more rigid coils. 'How did you come to be entrapped?'

'I've always been susceptible to the beauties of nature,' he replied. 'Nature knows it, and takes advantage. I heard your utterance – that

the hanging blossoms were something like wisteria and something
not – and I was trying to decide what they were most *not* like. It
was either a raven or a writing desk. As I paused to decide, nature
got the better of me. There, you are a brave young gentleman. I'm
sorry for any damage to your skirts. Your wife must send the bill
to my accountant. My solicitors will counter-sue. The whole merry
game will begin again. I am the White Knight, by the way.'

'I am Ada. I am looking for my friend, named Alice. I have
no wife. I am no gentleman.'

'Oh, you protest, but quality will out, sir. Look what a comfort
you're being.'

Ada had freed his arms. He helped her pick at the thickest parts
of the vine around his legs. Eventually he was able to pull his feet
out of his metal shoes, leaving them trapped. His stockings were in
need of a good rinsing. But he wrenched two bunches of drooping
flowers from the nearby vines. He thrust a foot into the midst of
each of them. They looked like festive, silvery lilac footwear, more
suitable for a visit to the baths than to a court of arbitrage.

'Given your armour, I assume you're a knight with a *K*.'

'Sometimes,' he said, 'though I have lost my helmet and visor.
For all I know I have misplaced the *K* in my name, too. But I
would answer to a White Night, sans the *K,* without blushing.'

'Night as in night-time? I never heard of a White Night.'

'The more common name of that animal, I believe, is Noon.'

'But there is no night-time in Noon.'

'Ah yes,' he said, sadly and kindly, 'the elderly militia know
that there is, there always is. One can die at any moment, you
see. Noon is a disguise of whiteness put on by the eternal Night
behind it.'

He was old. She didn't want him to talk about death. 'Here
is your helmet.' As she picked it up from the ferns, a feathery
white plume at its crest detached. It flew itself away, looking for
all the world like an escaping moustache.

'My love to your devoted mother,' cried the Knight to his plume. To Ada, he said, 'That's a fine valet I have, none better. But you've been a good lad, too. I shall put in for a promotion to the Queen. Very likely you shall be made Sergeant-at-the-Lower-Extremities, as you helped release my legs and feet.'

'I doubt it,' said Ada.

'Well, they already have a Sergeant-at-Arms, as far as I've heard. In any case, the Queen will decide. She always does.'

'Are you on your way to see the Queen?' asked Ada.

'In a manner of speaking,' said the old man, looking about dubiously. 'That is, I go out of my way *not* to see the Queen, as she has quite a temper, but I am rarely successful.'

'I had heard the Queen was temperate,' said Ada.

'Ill-tempered, temperate, a distinction without a difference,' said the Knight. 'As *illiterate* can refer to a cat who refuses to deliver a litter of kittens and instead delivers newspapers it has no capacity to read.'

'Ill-tempered and temperate *are* most certainly different states. They are opposites.'

'The Queen has become quite ravelled over the theft of her tarts,' insisted the Knight. 'And you know what *that* means.'

'No.'

'It means unravelled. I rest my case.'

Ada did not care to be rude. Still, she insisted, 'Opposites cannot mean the same thing.'

'Do you cleave to your belief about that?'

'Of course, or I shouldn't have made the remark.'

'Then cleave yourself from your beliefs. It's much of a muchness, or such of a suchness.'

'Well,' said Ada, 'in *any* case, I've never known an illiterate cat!'

'Don't become ravelled or unravelled over it. Sir, shall we go?'

Ada took his arm, as he seemed a bit wobbly on his pins. They made their way through the underbrush. 'I have always heard that Queen Victoria was moderate in her tastes,' ventured Ada.

'I never heard that at all,' replied the Knight. 'Then, I have never heard of Queen Victoria.'

'But you mentioned the ill-temper of the Queen.'

'I was referring to the Queen of Hearts,' he replied. 'Ever since her tarts were stolen clean away, she's been in a foul disposition. No one wants to attend her *fête* today, but if everyone sent in regrets she'd be left alone on the playing ground. She'd have to call for her own head to be cut off.'

'That sounds rather extreme.'

'She never earned high marks for civility, I'm afraid. She's ruthless, though great fun at a beheading. Now, for whom did you say you were looking?'

Ada kept nearly forgetting. 'Alice, a little girl. Like me. I believe she came this way, or nearby. Have you seen her?'

'I have never seen a little girl. I wouldn't recognize one if she stepped on me.'

'I'm a little girl,' she replied.

'If you're a little girl, I'll be a monkey's aunt.' He took off a thick leathern glove and fished about in his breastplate. He withdrew a magnifying glass on a chain, which he put to his eye. A glaucous eye, and runny. 'Well, timber my shivers, what an odd element you are,' he said. 'A most unconvincing-looking gentleman to stride the meadows. But then, the code of manliness requires us not to make comments on the intolerable ugliness of others. So I shall say no more about your condition, sir. But I do hope you manage to find some professional help. The bow in your hair is lopsided. Shall I?'

'I'll manage,' said Ada. 'I could never fix it myself before this, for my arms would not go all the way up and around. I too wore an iron armature, you see. Not unlike yours, though more private. I seem to have lost it.'

'I would lose my own suit of armour, though the Brigade to Preserve Morals in the Wilderness would probably have something to say about my choice of drawers. I favour an India-printed pattern of capering codfish. Are you going as far as the Queen's garden?'

Ada said, 'I never know where anything begins and ends here. So I don't know quite where I am going. But I am looking for Alice.'

'So you said. Well, if I should come across another gentleman kitted out as nonconformistly as you are, I shall ask if he is Alice. If he answers "Yes," he may be lying, so I shall pay no attention. If he answers "No," he may also be lying, so I shall send him directly to you with my compliments. What address shall I use?'

'I have no address,' she said. 'So I may as well continue along with you. Perhaps we shall find her together.'

'You have no chattel, no impedimenta,' observed the White Knight. 'I presume you have come to stay?'

She didn't know the answer. She'd embarked upon her unexpected journey without luggage of any variety, if one discounted the pot of marmalade. She felt only distant associations with the world of her dropsical mother and her father the Vicar, of Boykin Boyce the Screaming Wonder of the Nursery, and of Miss Armstrong Headstrong. Yet mentioning Alice to the old Knight made her friend come alive in Ada's thoughts, much as the unexpected whiff of balsam sap can revive all manner of Yuletide memories and hopes.

It occurred to Ada that Alice might be having a more difficult time of it in this peculiar wilderness than she was herself. She began to draw a distinction between them.

Ada had only one friend, and that was Alice. The Croft, where Alice's family lived, was near enough the Bickerage that Ada, chaperoned, could walk there by the river path, avoiding the crowds of Carfax or the High in Oxford proper. It was an untroubled route. In the centre of town, Ada was too likely to be jostled by hurrying dons or by housemaids with paper packets of suet tied with string. Or she might be stared at, which was another sort of annoyance.

Calm Alice never stared balefully at Ada, but talked and played in her own lively way. She included Ada when Ada turned up at the gate, but she ran off to follow a calf or a honeybee if it sang out to her, forgetting to bid Ada 'Goodbye!' or to say 'I'll return presently!' If Ada lived in portable iron stocks, Alice lived in the portable moment. They were well suited to be friends with each other. But if less constrained by the world than Ada was, Alice was also less tethered. Up until now.

Ada had been relieved of her exoskeleton. She was walking about with the freedom – well, the freedom of a young gentleman, actually. Perhaps that is what the old Knight was seeing in her, a jolly liberty, a certain being at-large. Whereas Alice, who knew? Through this unreliable landscape Alice might herself still be moving. Blundering, with no sense of direction, no recollection of her origins. It is what made Alice amazing, and also why she tended to get lost. She needed Ada, even if she didn't know it. It was Ada who would bring her home, if it could be managed.

'This wood is becoming insistent,' said the Knight. He took out his sword and tried to prise a space between the tree trunks. They were growing closer together. On all sides the gloom thickened. The voluted bark pressed in. The forest seemed more like a panelled chamber than a dense glade. As the Knight drew his sword back, breathing heavily, he knocked over a glass-topped table. A teacup fell and shattered on the marble floor, which was tiled like a chessboard in alternating squares of black and white. 'I say, sir,' he said to Ada, 'is that a keyhole I spy in yon chestnut bole? If so, would that key on the chain around your manly neck insert itself usefully therein?'

CHAPTER 21

The sun dispensed the sort of heat that presses against the skin and makes it itch. Lydia allowed her shawl to fall to her elbows. She was sorry she had brought it, but she had to have something to fiddle with. Her hands rarely knew how to keep still.

They had reached the banks of the Cherwell. A skirting of plummy black shadow was dropped below each exhausted riverbank tree. A few cows were standing hock-deep in the shallows, perhaps mesmerized by their reflections. Siam was flying at the water's edge and beginning to splash, as if he were in Brighton. Noon bells sang out with their usual ignorance of mood, marking out moments of grief and worry, elation and confusion. The bells said that at its core, human life was fundamentally a sort of organic clockwork, while the winds and skylarks that swept against the sound of metronomic iron timekeeping argued for variety, subtlety, epiphany. What the sun thought, or meant, or said, was too high overhead to be heard. Like the vasty deity to which Lydia's father tried to pray, the sun shouted its light and simultaneously kept its magnificent silence.

What *might* her mother have made of Mr Winter? It was a question that Lydia could neither answer nor let go. Against her reservations she forced herself to think in the funereal subjunctive. How *would* Mama have proceeded to chat with this unexpected American visitor?

Mrs Clowd might not have waited for Pater to introduce the guest. Mrs Clowd would have exchanged pleasantries at the outset. She'd have spoken with a lively good humour, at once teasing and tender, asking droll questions that could summon no sensible reply. Mrs Clowd would have embarrassed her husband, who would have been happy to be embarrassed. Mrs Clowd dashed a room with fancy. Mrs Clowd was dead. What lesson here for Lydia?

Josiah Winter seemed satisfied to stroll in silence. He clasped his hands behind his back. Lydia didn't have her mother's bravado. As she understood the protocol, Lydia must wait until Mr Winter felt ready to speak again. She couldn't imagine how she might bring herself to address him first. She pictured, mostly in fun, how she might stumble so he would have to reach out a steadying hand. Though he was an American, surely he would be at least *that* gallant?

'As we weren't presented to each other formally,' said Mr Winter at last, 'I haven't had the occasion to express my condolences on the loss of your mother.'

She was so relieved he'd spoken at last that she had to clutch her stomach muscles with her hands. *Oh, we never lost her; we know precisely the plot of ground in which her coffin was laid.* To keep from saying that, she began to giggle. But humour is anarchic. She snorted. Her nose blew out and her eyes ran. *Losing your mother.* Wasn't that exactly what Pater wanted and needed, to revoke that loss, to correct that error of misplacing someone for eternity? And Pater required the reassurance of Darwin himself, of all people. Pater required some declaration of persisting faith, so that as Jane Isabel Clowd, late of this parish and removed to Iffley churchyard, drew further away in time and in memory from her husband and daughters, the chances of her salvation and of the resurrection of her soul should not be equally adrift.

For time had changed its terms, no matter what the bells of Oxford said. The one-sided eternity of the afterlife, only a few years after the Oxford Debate, was now guessed to have a secret twin, a mirrored flank, beginning, if eternities could begin, as long a time before a life as the Scriptures proposed it would continue after.

'Oh, Miss Lydia,' said Mr Winter. He pulled from a waistcoat pocket a clean handkerchief. 'I have upset you, when I meant only to console you.'

'It is the silly pollen,' she cried. She accepted his attentions and wiped her eyes. 'The great Darwin himself cannot cozen my father back into his faith. The lock has sprung and it will not hitch again.'

'Your father is a brave man. He seems to be an honest one. I mean honest in his mind,' he continued. 'I mean in his *thinking*. I am not saying this at all well.'

'Pater says it ought not to make a difference if man's place in nature, as Mr Darwin recently insists, has a different origin than we understood before. Do you know what I mean?'

'I have heard Mr Darwin use the phrase "the descent of man",' remarked Josiah Winter.

She frowned. 'Some days I do not know how much further down we could go.'

'Those are dark words for a young lady as pretty as you. Darwin doesn't mean those words in a spiritual or moral sense, but only in terms of our history as primates. You are descended from your parents. It is *that* use of the word he means to imply.'

'If we concede a different past, must we conclude a different future?' protested Lydia.

'That's your father's question. I see that. And made intense by the loss of his wife, whom I wish I had had the fortune to meet. But you must not take upon yourself your father's struggle. Remember your own English hymn, so popular in my country and, I believe, sung at the funeral of your Prince Albert. "Rock of Ages." It has the most encouraging conclusion.'

The stranger then began to sing, right out in the open air.

> 'While I draw this fleeting breath,
> When mine eyes shall close in death,
> When I soar to worlds unknown,
> See Thee on Thy judgment throne,
> Rock of Ages, cleft for me,
> Let me hide myself in Thee.'

Lydia hardly knew what to say. She supposed she had asked for this. Soaring to worlds unknown sounded like an ascent, but becoming a plug in the Rock of Ages was surely not a celestial event, but a granitic one, the sepulchral descent of man.

She didn't know if she should return his handkerchief, damp as it was. But he might think she was clinging to it as a souvenir. Perhaps she would do just that. 'He's getting a good deal ahead,' she managed, pointing at Siam.

'I will not lose him. I am all he has.'

'He is lucky, I suppose.'

'I do not think often about luck, except the quirk of accident that brought his soul into the world as a Negro in Georgia, and mine as a white man in the Commonwealth of Massachusetts.'

'I should have imagined that was no accident.' Lydia attempted a sweetness that was, perhaps, not entirely successful. 'Don't you think, rather, the Almighty decides, at His sacred whim, which of us shall ascend and which descend? Shan't we pay homage to His mastery by enduring the circumstances of our lives?'

He didn't speak for a while. He smiled at her sideways, quizzically. Then he said, 'I see you are your father's daughter, possessed of a quick mind. What a pity that, with all these great chapels of learning tottering about on every side of you, you will not have a chance to argue with some dean of divinity.'

'We must conclude that my gender is another decision of the Almighty,' she said. Her tone was more muted. 'I don't discuss such matters with my father, though I listen when he speaks. Upon occasion, Pater tutors local grammar school boys hoping to sit the exams. He is especially interested in biblical history.'

'I'm surprised he doesn't teach at one of the colleges.'

'We're not all equally gifted,' was all she would say. 'He enjoys his work in the archives of the Bodleian. He absorbs whatever he can by glancing at the volumes he locates for the scholars, who require them for their study.'

'An education in scraps and moments.'

'All that is afforded most of us. Did you attend a college, Mr Winter?'

Before he could answer, a fluting voice hailed Lydia from across the rich meadow. Miss Armstrong was bowling along, carrying a parasol to protect her noble nose from the sunlight. 'Oh, Miss Lydia, how glad I am to see you again,' she cried. 'I must confer with you, if you can spare me the time.'

The governess descended upon them, huffing. 'The descent of woman,' muttered Lydia. She was certain that Mr Winter had not heard her.

CHAPTER 22

The key that the rattled Hare had given Ada: would it fit in the door? It would. Would it swivel in the lock? Indeed it would, with a self-satisfied and industrious little click.

But then, would the door open?

This was a different matter. Though the key had turned, the brass doorknob would not. Ada looked at the words engraved on its shiny surface. They were even smaller than before. She had to kneel and put her face close to the doorknob to try to make them out.

'I left my spectacles on the mantelpiece, little man. What does it say?' asked the White Knight.

'I think it says ALL YE WHO ENTER HERE, ABANDON HOPE,' replied Ada, 'though I can't be sure. The letters are *very* small and imprecise.'

'I suspect its advice is to abandon *home*,' said the Knight. 'As it turns out, I left home this morning. I refused to bring it along however much it whined. I believe I am qualified for admittance. Step away, let me try the door.'

'It was my key,' said Ada, perhaps sullenly.

'Ah, but you have not abandoned quite enough home,' said the White Knight. 'You are a very young gentleman. Some habits are hard to shake off until you are old and frail like me. I have shaken off romance, ambition and curly locks along with the accoutrements of the domestic life. I will not be denied. Aside, I say.'

She moved aside. The White Knight took off his glove. He tried the doorknob. It would not turn. He tried to push the door in with his shoulder, but he could not budge it. He tried to pull it. Since he had braced his feet against the door for leverage, this proved a doomed strategy.

'Perhaps if we both pushed at once,' he said. Ada returned to her position. Unaccustomed to being asked to perform physical assistance of any sort, she was pleased. 'On the count of three, we shall rush at the door with all our might,' he said. 'Five, four, three.'

They both hurtled themselves forwards. A curious thing happened then. The door opened, but not by swinging wide, as a book swings open on its hinged spine. Instead, fixed upon a central horizontal axis, the door behaved like a flywheel. The top half fell inward. The White Knight tumbled head-first through the doorway like a sack of chain-mail laundry tossed in a chute. At the same time, the bottom half of the door kicked up and outwards. Ada was struck in the elbows and knees. She tumbled backwards as the White Knight fell forwards. She righted herself in time to see his heels disappear behind the closing door, which slammed shut with a snap that had a vindictive character to it.

The door had revolved. There was still a keyhole, but no key dangled from it. The key was stuck in the keyhole on the other side. The door was locked again. Ada went on her knees once more to try to peer through the keyhole, to call to the Knight, to tell him to open the door from that side. But the keyhole was blocked by the key. She could see nothing more of the serene garden, the Knight, the roses, or the playing cards setting up for the grand *fête*.

She stood up. The letters on the doorknob were scrambling about to form a new message. She didn't care to read depressing messages. She turned away from it.

The panelled hall was a forest again, but a dull, cloistered sort of forest. Gone were the hot spots of green and gold that sunlight loves to scatter as a corrective against boskiness. Yet it didn't feel like evening. It took Ada a moment to realize that she was a little clammy. A mist had begun to seep through the woods. Had she wanted to backtrack towards the Hatter and the Hare at their tea party, she wouldn't have known which way to go. Moisture was collecting on her skin and her upper lip the way it did when fog crept in at the seaside. She had no shawl. For warmth, she began to walk through the gloom, swinging her arms martially as any perfect little soldier might do.

The mist curled and tried to rub against her, but she wouldn't let it touch. She kept up her spirits by reciting certain nursery plaints that Miss Armstrong had been accustomed to delivering in regretful tones.

> 'Little Jack Horner and Little Boy Blue
> Fell into trouble and sank in the stew.
> Old Mother Hubbard soon had the pot covered
> And served them for supper. Her dog had some, too.'

That did not sound entirely as it ought. She tried again.

> 'Little Miss Muffet and Mary Contrary
> Found in the garden a spider most scary.
> It stung them and hung them to save them for dinner,
> A fate that awaits the conventional sinner.'

She hadn't recalled that the nursery characters knew one another so well. Nor that they were all so bent on dining.

She hurried along the path, thinking that the fog itself was like a toothless mouth trying to close upon her. A mouth without a body attached. But how odd – she never thought in sloppy images like this.

> *'Robin a'Bobbin, a big-bellied wren*
> *Ate more meat than forty men can.*
> *He ate a church, he ate a steeple,*
> *He opened the doors and gobbled the people.*
> *He ate the future and the past,*
> *And all the days as they galloped past.*
> *He ate the prophets, stars and sky,*
> *And fell down dead and refused to die.'*

'I am beginning to feel I grew up in the wrong nursery, as these rhymes won't behave,' she said aloud, to give herself courage. 'I wonder if nursery rhymes do lasting damage?' Before she could answer her own question, the path dropped in a steep decline. She found herself rushing downslope into a clearing in the mist. Her new agility failed her. She tumbled.

A group of travellers turned to her. 'Oh, my, a guardian angel,' cried one. 'How welcome, for we are quite lost. I fear we will arrive late for our performance.'

Ada drew herself up short. The figure addressing her was flat and sharp, possibly cut out of a sheet of metal and painted in carnival colours. A Tin Ballerina, with one leg lifted and a beribboned tambourine pinched in her tin fingers. She was accompanied by a Tin Bear with a valise upon his upturned nose. Sauntering along behind was a large, sour-looking, fully ovoid Egg, wearing a necktie and little else.

'What a remarkable family you have,' said Ada to the Tin Ballerina.

'We have no family, we simply have careers. We are in the theatre,' replied the Tin Ballerina, a little sadly.

'I thought there seemed a bit of Punch and Judy to you. Where are you going?'

'We are going to perform, of course, but we have lost our way in this purgatorial soup. You are good to show up and lead us forwards, you heavenly creature.'

'I am not that good,' said Ada. 'And I am not a guardian angel.'

'You came from above, didn't you? That's the origin of angels,' replied the Tin Ballerina.

Ada didn't know if the Tin Ballerina was referring to the slope or to the world of upper Oxford. 'Well. I came from above. Yes. But only in a manner of speaking.'

'She has no strings,' said the Tin Bear. 'She's a guardian angel, all right.'

'No one asks me my opinion,' snapped the Egg, 'but if they should, I might have something sharp to say!'

'Dear Humpty Dumpty, what is your opinion?' asked the Tin Ballerina.

'I have no idea,' he replied. 'Perhaps she is a guardian orna-ment, intended to revolve in the wind like other tin weather-vanes.' Oh, thought Ada, *that's* what the Tin Bear and the Tin Ballerina most resemble: weather-vanes. While the Egg resembled nothing so much as a refugee from a luncheon platter.

'You're players meant to entertain at the garden party of the Queen of Hearts!' guessed Ada.

'If you say so,' said the Tin Bear. '*I* would have said we were cheap ornaments intended for the decoration of joyless holiday endeavour, destined for the rubbish bin, but you know best, dear guardian angel.'

'Please don't think me a guardian angel. For one thing—'

'You are hardly a guardian mongoose,' said Humpty Dumpty. 'And a good thing, too, for mongooses eat raw eggs.'

'Alas,' said the Tin Bear, 'guardian angel or not, you cannot join our band. You have no strings. So you are not a marionette.'

'*You* have no strings,' said Ada. 'If I am not a guardian angel, neither are you marionettes. I think you're weather-vanes. I mean, except Mr Egg.'

'We are poor soothsayers, I'm afraid. We cannot tell whether the weather will hold for the party,' said the Tin Ballerina. 'In any case, we do have strings. I don't mean in *any* case, really, I mean in *that* case.' She revolved upon her toe so her extended leg pointed toward the valise balanced atop the Tin Bear. 'We keep them coiled in the satchel until they are needed. Now, tell us whether or not you are going to guide us to the party.'

Ada said, 'If you are weather-vanes, you ought to be able to sort out your location from which way the fog is blowing in. No?'

'I thought I told you. We're whether-vanes, with an *h*,' said the Tin Ballerina. 'We don't know whether we're coming or going. It's supposed to be charming, but it makes our professional appearances alarmingly impromptu.'

Ada put a finger to her lips. 'Aren't *you* a guardian Egg?' she asked the one called Humpty Dumpty. 'I had been told a Head Egg like you was serving as a lookout to protect birds' nests from hungry serpents.'

'I've been told *you* went out walking in the lane without a chaperone!' he retorted. 'Mind your own business. I left the position of guardian Egg to take up a higher calling. Art is all. You will rarely have seen a performance in which an Egg has such an exalted role.'

'I've never seen any performance in which an Egg was featured at all,' admitted Ada.

'Exactly,' said Humpty Dumpty. 'I rest my case.'

'I wish I could rest *my* case,' said the Tin Bear. His valise was soldered to his nose.

'Prepare to be astounded,' continued Humpty Dumpty to Ada. 'If we ever get there, I mean.'

'Perhaps I could join your troupe. I should like to go to the garden party, too,' said Ada. 'I am hunting for a friend, you see. I'm afraid that she may be lost.'

'She's no more lost than Paradise,' said the Tin Bear. Everyone looked at him. 'Do you think even Paradise Lost could find itself in this fog? *Really.*'

'Well, we can't get any more lost than we are,' decided Ada. 'So I'll come along with you. We'll see where we get.'

'That will never do,' said the Tin Ballerina. '*We'll* come along with *you,* and we'll see where we get.'

The Egg muttered something bitter that Ada couldn't quite catch. Then that noise, like the ongoing collapse of an industrial artifact, sounded again, and too near for comfort. Without choosing a path, they all ran in single file: Ada first, the Tin Ballerina hopping *en pointe,* the Tin Bear stumping behind. Humpty Dumpty was last, glancing over the great flanks of his even jowls (he had no shoulders to speak of). The forest grew indistinct with fog. The leafy branches of trees seemed like great mittened claws eager to scrape at the party. It couldn't be denied that the clangorous monster was following them. 'The Jabberwock!' hissed the Tin Bear. 'A Guardian Demon!' They all closed their eyes as they ran. The fog was so close they couldn't see more than a foot ahead of themselves anyway.

CHAPTER 23

The governess again! A riverbank nixie gone mad for interruption into human affairs. Puck's countervalence. Lydia could spit. But the manifestation of Miss Armstrong snapped Lydia to attention. So far, Mr Josiah Winter had proven little more than an unexpected aspect of Lydia's morning. If, in time to come, this June day would be picked out in her memory for special notice, it would be because she had strolled upon the riverbank with a young American gentleman. True, their duet of comments and potent pauses had been only an experiment at grown-up conversation. But they *were* together as a pair, strolling. A first, for Lydia.

With Miss Armstrong hieing into view, however, the dalliance of this walk, the private silly adventure of it, was now beaten into something public and coarse. This encounter on the Cherwell bank would lie between Lydia and Miss Armstrong, unmentioned, every time their paths crossed for the rest of their lives.

She glared at Miss Armstrong swooping across the meadow, cutting the diagonal the more quickly to meet them. Miss Armstrong was watching where she placed her feet. She didn't notice Lydia's ferocity. And Lydia thought: the court and the rabble of Athens move so quickly into the woods, stung and shifted by magic, abused by Puck. Shakespeare was showing how any social event is composed of separate simultaneous experiences, whose meanings differ, and must be negotiated into commonality if history is to occur.

She had no intention of negotiating with Miss Armstrong, but Lydia was stuck like a wasp in honey. The stroll was no longer hers alone. Hers, and Mr Winter's.

'I was hoping to waylay you, Miss Lydia,' huffed Miss Armstrong. She put out her hand to grasp Lydia by the wrist, in friendship or worry. Lydia offered no wrist. After a moment Mr Winter held out his hand. Miss Armstrong recoiled with flare, as if she hadn't noticed the gentleman till his hand appeared. 'Begging your pardon, sir; I am interrupting your meander. I am—'

'Mr Winter, may I present Miss Armstrong,' said Lydia. It was not a question. 'A governess from the Vicarage along the way.' The tone in which she said *governess* had a likeness to iron.

'How do you do.' Mr Winter bowed from the waist.

Rallying, Miss Armstrong became downright Bohemian. 'Miss Lydia, the Vicarage has gone turnips to toast! Ada has not returned, but that's the least of it. The infant is squalling as if being pricked with invisible needles. The doctor has been sent for. Mrs Boyce has taken the boy to her bosom. She has turned the Vicar out of the sewing room. He is *beside* himself, and you know what he is *like*!'

Lydia had no idea what the Vicar was like. She was not interested in learning. She couldn't decipher this story, with its needles and bosoms and squallings. Oh, so the infant had the hiccups. To judge by the look on Miss Armstrong's face, the Pennines would now collapse and the Hebrides float away towards Norway. But all this drama couldn't deter Lydia from her obligations, much as she tried to resist them. 'Miss Armstrong, this is Mr Winter, lately of London though originating in those pestered States across the ocean.'

'I understand,' said Miss Armstrong in a tone of regret. She put a hand to her bonnet brim as if to brush away a horsefly. 'Miss Lydia, I am beside myself.'

'So I see,' said Lydia. 'I have no words of advice for you, though. We are engaged in our own campaigns. We're out looking for Alice, as she hasn't returned either. No one has reached a state of alarm, mind you. Alice never goes far. She merely goes . . .' She thought. 'Deep.'

Miss Armstrong murmured, 'Where is the boy who looks after the sheep, but under the haystack, fast asleep.' They began to walk together, a hateful trio.

'I know that nursery ditty,' said Mr Winter. 'It is sung at the cots of Concord babes. Interesting how the word *fast* suggests, in that instance, a way of holding. From the word *fastened,* I suppose. Locked in sleep, kept.'

'Is it possible that Ada is locked in sleep somewhere with her head on Alice's shoulder?' said Miss Armstrong. 'Has *anyone* seen Ada today?'

'One might imagine she'd been pushed into the river and drowned, to simplify her life and everyone else's,' said Lydia.

'No one could imagine such a thing,' protested Miss Armstrong.

'You did,' said Lydia. 'You told me earlier. You pictured Ada fetched up against the milldam, as I re—'

'The marmalade—'

'Ada and her marmalade!' Lydia made an airy, dismissive sound like a French laundress. How Miss Armstrong could jabber as she walked! 'Miss Lydia, Ada can't have gone far. But some forbidden destination would have appealed to her more strongly than the company of Alice.' In an aside to Mr Winter, Lydia said, 'My sister isn't always attentive. Oh, she's never unkind, but she's easily distractible. If she and Ada were playing a game of hide-and-seek, and Ada had closed herself in a wardrobe, Alice might decide to go and dig worms in the garden and drop them in the well. Ada could spend the day waiting to be found.'

'Don't say that!' Miss Armstrong took a fright. 'Mr Winter, Ada Boyce has never gone out alone before today. It's always been my pleasure to walk with her endlessly, endlessly, hither and yon, *endlessly,* but what with turmoil at home, Ada escaped me. The Vicar – oh, possessed of such piety!' She shook her head; her shoulders wobbled, too. 'And Mrs Boyce, distracted by the nuisance of a newborn, and all her natural feeling for her husband channelled elsewhere. It is a harlequinade, a harlequinade enacted in a torched and smoking rectory, by people devastated with terror and Madeira.' She had said too much, of course, she had flung her*self* into the river and drowned. She blinked two or three times like a Guernsey surprised to have just delivered an aria. She lowered her parasol, closed it. She stabbed the ground with it as if to kill the very earth upon which she walked. She lifted both hands in a gesture of defeat that didn't fool Lydia for a moment. 'I am not myself today,' said Miss Armstrong by way of apology, in a softer tone.

'Few are,' said Mr Winter. Lydia couldn't tell if he was being amusing or rude. 'Of course, we'll look for your Ada while we keep an eye out for Miss Lydia's sister. Would you care to walk along with us?'

Lydia couldn't bear it. 'I suspect, Miss Armstrong, that having escaped you, Ada took the chance to engage a boatman to take her across the river. I seem to think she said something of the sort. To explore the other side, she said. And look, there's a boatman lolling down on that spit. Just there. Perhaps you should hire him yourself, and go and have a look around that side of the river. We'll check out this side. One *never knows.*' The tone was ominous. 'Of course if we find Ada we'll send her home at once. I have already told you that, Miss Armstrong.'

But now Miss Armstrong was weeping. Lydia could have given her a good hard kick. 'I can't begin to tell you what it would mean – to us – if I were sent away!' she sobbed. Mr Winter stopped, pale. Had he never encountered a volatile woman before? He put out his hand and settled it upon Miss Armstrong's shoulder. She couldn't look up, but she raised one hand and rested it upon his as if they had known one another for twenty years. The bells began to sound the quarter hour. The sun blinked behind a cloud. For a moment the colours took on a hasty intensity. The first cloud after a session of blinding sunlight is a shade of the underworld, a hint of the grave and even how it might smell. Lydia felt a shiver of dread, but overcame it.

'I understand what you feel,' said Mr Winter. 'Should anything happen to my lad, I would be beside myself.'

'Your lad,' chimed Miss Armstrong questioningly.

'Siam.' Lydia spoke with a ferocious oratorical clarity. 'Ahead of us on the path. Halloo, Siam!' she called to the boy, who turned and waved.

Miss Armstrong lost some ground. It was too much. 'You may be right,' she said to someone, to herself. Who knew what she meant? She pivoted away from the riverbank path and began beating down the shallow slope to the water's edge. Lydia turned her shoulder; the subject was closed. As the moment passed, the dome of the Radcliffe Camera in the distance came out of shadow into the sun. The stodgy beauties of the colleges, and all these comic barbarians at their finialed gates.

'What a passionate creature,' said Mr Winter.

'She's an utter lunatic.'

'But look, she's left behind her parasol. She'll need it, with the sun on the water. Miss Armstrong,' he called, with what Lydia thought was perhaps not a full-throated effort. Distance, and the noise of the governess's rushing skirts, must have kept her from hearing. 'I shall go after her and deliver it,' he decided. 'I shall ambush her by the launch, hand her the thing, and return, like so. Keep on along the riverbank.' He indicated with a nod of his head a path ahead by which he'd come back to Lydia. 'I shall rejoin you along the way, having made a triangle of it. With your permission.'

Lydia didn't give permission, but he was off on his own, gambolling like an idiotic April lamb. She didn't want to witness the reunion from this distance, any distance. She suspected he would loiter. She hated him, she hated them both. She turned her face into the wind. She looked for black Siam, a sentimental silhouette against the diamond-dashed glitter and glare of a backwash of the Cherwell. She cupped her hands at her mouth. 'I say,' she called to him, at a volume she knew the adults couldn't hear. 'We're told to head back. Come with me.'

CHAPTER 24

We must now, if only for a moment, consider Siam on the riverbank, and what he sees. He examines life as intently as anyone else in this history. That the puzzlingly kind Mr Josiah is loping along the bank, away from him – this causes in Siam a mix of relief and anxiety at the same instant. And what of Miss Lydia, the half-adult missie, with her flaxen hair pulled forward in a way that fails to disguise the vastness of her forehead? She puts Siam in mind of the white cliffs of Albion, as Mr Josiah had named them, on the vessel that brought them from Oostende.

Persons like Miss Lydia are an unknown element in Siam's life. His experience with white females of that age has been so chaperoned as to kill conversation. He doesn't think in terms of vixen, virago or virgin. He thinks she is attractive, though perhaps an aberration, like one of those new barnacles or orchids about which Mr Josiah has yammered with Mr Darwin. They broke the mould before they cast her, he thinks. That is perhaps not quite right. Still, it seems fitting.

Of Miss Armstrong he has no opinion. She is a wild improbability whom he can see but has not met. He watched Mr Josiah loping down a sloping bank towards her. Miss Lydia is hollering something to Siam. He ventures a few feet nearer to see if he can understand her words beneath her accent.

CHAPTER 25

The woods began to thin. The sound of hastening footsteps in the fog took on sloshy echo. They were running through marsh grass now, wetlands. Their feet were soaked. Perhaps we are at the side of the ocean, thought Ada. 'The salt air will do you no good,' she panted to the Tin Ballerina and the Tin Bear. 'You will come down with a pox.'

'I adore salt,' huffed Humpty Dumpty. 'Salt completes me.'

'We mustn't plunge into the sea or we would have to consider drowning,' said the Tin Bear. 'And I'm not sure I'm capable of that. I'd be an utter failure.'

The noise of their pursuer only intensified. They heard a hunger in that racket, or some other ambition. The Jabberwock, if such it was, must be lost in the fog, too. They cringed at the creak and clang of its limbs, which seemed in the thickening air to be all around them.

'We are but poor players a-wandering in the muck and the mire,' said the Tin Ballerina. 'It's time we relied upon a higher power. We must put ourselves in the hands of loftier management.'

'All right,' said the Tin Bear. He unfolded from his valise a baker's dozen of brightly coloured kites, in patterns of red and black and white. Each had a string attached to one corner. The Tin Bear tied the other ends of the strings to various limbs of the travelling troupe.

'I'm afraid we don't have any extras,' said the Tin Ballerina

to Ada. 'But you may hold my hand for comfort and guidance,
if you like. Perhaps you will be lifted up by our society.'

'There does not seem to be much uplift in my day today,'
said Ada, 'but I'm willing to try.'

'Good. You run ahead. When the wind catches the kite, launch
it,' said the Tin Ballerina.

'How do you do this when you're all alone?' she asked.

'Privately,' said the Tin Ballerina. 'Run!'

Ada ran. When the string stretched taut and a wind came up,
she tossed the kite up into the fog. Before it rose and disappeared
into the mist, it turned once or twice. The kite was made of a
playing card.

'That was a Three of Diamonds,' she shouted to the troupe
of players.

'The sky is improved by additional diamonds,' said Humpty
Dumpty. 'Next kite, hurry! That creature is getting closer.'

It took only a few moments before all thirteen kites were
launched. They disappeared into the low cloud cover. Ada now
saw that the creatures had been transformed into marionettes.
The tin cutouts and Humpty Dumpty were each suspended a
few feet in the air by four kite-card strings. Humpty clenched
the string to the Ace between his teeth, perhaps because he was
top-heavy.

'We are now in fine hands,' said the Tin Ballerina, glancing
skywards.

'My hand is finer than yours,' mumbled Humpty Dumpty. 'I
have a royal flush.'

'Oh,' said the Tin Bear to Ada, 'I forgot; we do have one
final kite. We rarely use it, but you are welcome to it if you like.
It is a Joker.'

'Ah.' Ada wasn't sure if this was a good idea. It seemed impo-
lite to turn the offer down, though, so she launched herself a
kite. She gripped the string as the wind began to lead them in

a direction that had no whether-or-not to it. They weren't lifted far off the ground but skipped and hopped as marionettes do, untroubled by gravity, drawn by strings directing them from the sky.

'How do you know this is the right way?' she asked.

'We do not question our higher power,' said Humpty Dumpty. 'It knows best.'

'We are but tugged at the whim of the Creator,' agreed the Tin Bear.

'Though we struggle in fog, our fate is in the cards,' called the Tin Ballerina. And who knew but that she was right, for the sound of the menacing creature that pursued them began to recede a little. The kites dragged Ada, the Tin Ballerina, the Tin Bear and Humpty Dumpty so quickly that there was no more breath for talking. It reminded Ada of going for a walk with Miss Armstrong.

At length the mist began to dissipate. It seemed they must have covered many miles. The wind slackened. The kites drooped and failed. They found themselves pausing in a mature beech wood, right at the door of a small, stately home made of stone and, it seemed, crumpets and old boots.

They untied their strings and rolled them up, and they crammed the kites back in the valise of the Tin Bear. 'You are most admirable marionettes,' admitted Ada.

'We have no say in the matter,' said the Tin Ballerina, without remorse. 'Life blows us where it will. Hither, thither, and whether. We play our little witty roles. I should have liked to run a boardinghouse, but life has not given me that.'

'Hush,' said the Tin Bear. 'Is that the wind, or has the Terror of the Fog followed us even here?'

Sure enough, a strangled iron cry reverberated a good way off. If it had followed them this far, alas, it would come nearer. Ada rapped on the door, hoping for the best.

In short order the door was opened by a sleepy-looking housemaid in a mob-cap. 'They've all gone off,' she said grumpily. 'Go away.'

'They've gone, and we've come,' said the Tin Bear. 'Let us in.'

'I'm not scared of a dancing bear with a portmanteau stuck on his noddle,' said the housemaid, but she opened the door just the same. 'Very well, if there's no stopping you.'

'Who's gone off?' asked Ada as they crowded into the filthy kitchen. A pot of soup had bubbled down to grime and was gently scorching upon the hob.

'Why, the Duchess, of course, and the Cook. The Duchess went to the garden party in high dudgeon, but the Cook wasn't invited, so she went to her sister's in low spirits.'

'High Dudgeon and Low Spirits,' said Humpty Dumpty. 'Very fine addresses, both. I don't suppose you have a bite to offer us?'

'There's naught to eat, what with that pig about,' said the housemaid, 'so keep a proper tongue in your head or we'll see how large a *soufflé* you might make.' She sat on a stool and picked up her knitting. She seemed to be devising a morning coat out of seaweed.

A terrible roar, all too close, descended upon the house. Through the window they could see crumpets falling off the roof. A glory of soot emitted from the chimney. Ada and the marionettes clung to one another, but the housemaid only yawned. 'I wonder if that's the Baby wanting its brekky,' said the housemaid. 'Baby *likes* eggs.'

'I adore babies myself,' said Humpty Dumpty, flashing some pointy teeth.

'Is that the noise of the Jabberwock?' asked Ada.

'I couldn't say. I wouldn't know a Jabberwock from a Wockerjab. Could be Baby in a state. Perhaps Baby knows.' The housemaid opened a little iron door to a bread oven. A pig poked his head out the aperture.

'Is that you making such a horrid row?' asked the housemaid. The pig shook his snout. The stertorous commotion seemed to have landed on the eaves, as the room was showered with crumbs and dust. The housemaid said to the guests, 'Baby has a wicked chest cold, but that cough belongs to something else. Maybe that Jockerwab you was collecting, for a specimen, was it?'

'And what *is* a Jabberwock?' asked Ada.

At this the Baby turned his little snout up and rolled his little piggy eyes at her. He began to speak.

> *'And what's a Jabberwock, you ask?*
> *To answer is a gruesome task.*
> *It is not ape though ape it may.*
> *To be a bee it cannot be.*
> *"Not carp?" you carp; "Not carp," I say.*
> *Nor dog, though dogged, I decree.*
> *It is not ewe – how you amuse! –*
> *Nor fish, although you fish for clues—'*

'Intolerable nonsense,' interrupted Humpty Dumpty.

'You've ruined my line of thought,' snapped the Baby.

'Just finish up, and then we'll know what a Jabberwock truly is,' said Ada peaceably enough. 'Knowledge comes at the end.'

'The end part goes like this,' said the Baby sharply.

> *'The only sound it makes is sproink,*
> *And on the matter, by my bladder, that's my final*
> *oink.'*

Then the Baby wiggled out of the bread oven, fell on the floor, and turned and bit his own curly tail in annoyance.

'We didn't hear all the *other* animals it isn't,' said Ada. 'So how will we recognize it when we find it?'

'It'll find you,' said the Baby grimly, snuffling for crumbs under the pastry table.

'Does either of you know the way to the garden party?' said Ada. 'That's where we are headed. The marionettes are performing, and I am looking for a friend.'

'*You'll* never find a friend, not with that attitude!' said Humpty Dumpty.

The housemaid said to Ada, 'I'll show you how to get to the garden gate, though I'd not go inside myself. I'm not invited.'

'And a good thing, too,' said the Baby, eating a tea towel off the airing rack. '*You'd* bring the tone down, you would.'

'No sugar-water for you,' said the housemaid, 'if you're going to make personal remarks.'

'It's the only kind I know how to make.' The Baby began to run around the table, oinking up a storm. 'I think the Jabberwock is eating the roof! Everybody hide.'

'Quick,' said the housemaid. She stood and put on the seaweed jacket. It now seemed as broad as a cape, and somehow it was capacious enough for all of them to huddle under. Crumbs of plaster dust like caster sugar showered upon them as she drew the edges of the coat together. 'I always find if you're caught at home without a vorpal blade, a seaweed frock serves as a fine caution against germs and Jabberwocks.' She fastened a button somehow. They plunged into darkness.

# CHAPTER 26

Lydia had had no difficulty persuading Siam to return with her to the Croft. 'Your Mr Winter will find us there,' she said. 'He's on an errand of foolishness or mercy, or perhaps both.'

Siam made no reply. Perhaps, Lydia thought, that description characterizes Mr Winter's attention to Siam, too.

Lydia thought it wouldn't be proper for them to walk abreast, though she wasn't sure why. She pressed ahead, remarking over her shoulder, 'Mind the burrs,' and 'We'll turn here, it's quicker.' They passed into a grove of saplings. For a moment they were out of sight of any rooftops or chimney pots, cows or river. The June greenery gave off its smell of sour and sweet fervour. She almost felt drunk. How wild the world was, when you paused to look over the stile, out any window, across the herbaceous borders of propriety, 1860s version.

She stopped and turned, without forethought. She faced Siam. He had just leaped over a spot of puddle and so he was right at her chin. He couldn't back up because of the mud. She didn't retreat either.

'How do you find it, travelling about with him?' she said.

How fast the shutters flew up, how fast the curtains were drawn! A look of uncomprehending stiffness such as one might catch from a Welshman. Siam said, 'Mr Josiah he make all the bookings and such.'

'Tell me about where you were born. Tell me about your family.'

'Nothing to say 'bout that. It's all—' He made a gesture with his hand. 'All gone.'

'We have little in common, but we have that,' she said. 'My mother is gone, too. She died some months ago.'

He shrugged. She guessed that he knew there was nothing to say. They had nothing to give to each other. Grief cocoons the newly bereaved, and sometimes they never escape.

'I am going mad,' said Lydia. 'Always responsible for Alice, always tending to my desperate father. Neither the matron of the house nor the daughter.' Oh, but she was sounding like Miss Armstrong now. 'How do you manage, going from here to there? Are you escaping owners who would enslave you and bring you back to whichever southern state you fled from? Or do you have a destination? Is there a home for you ahead?'

'Mr Josiah my home,' he said. His eyes were glazed. He looked over Lydia's shoulder. A wind pushed the leaves about. It was like being swamped in a green tide rolling in.

'Are you being followed even in England?' she asked. He would not answer.

'You was looking for your sister,' he said at last.

'She can look after herself. She'll show up when she's hungry. I want to know more about Mr Winter.'

'I can't say. He away with that blue jay woman.'

She took that to be a caution. Calling Miss Armstrong a blue jay! 'Is he often scarpering off with single women?'

'Let's go.'

'I see,' she said. It wasn't so much pity as irritation that turned her heel once more. She heard in his avoidance of the subject something untoward about the character of Mr Winter. Her annoyance was shot through with a surge of bile and regret. The resulting admixture might have been called rage. She kept her voice still as a tyrant adult might. 'Very well. Back to the morgue.'

A tension had arisen between them. When he stopped to pick up a stone or a feather or whatever attracted him, she didn't wait. By the time she reached the Croft, he was quite a few steps behind. She didn't hold the gate.

'Well?' asked Mrs Brummidge.

'Alice is out larking somewhere with Ada Boyce, it seems. Miss Armstrong is rounding them up.'

'Quite right, too. And Mr Winter's young charge? What did you do with him?' Mrs Brummidge looked foul and censorious.

'What do you think I did? I slaughtered him and pushed him in the river.'

'You need a nostrum for your wild panics, my girl. But one distress at a time. Mr Darwin rang for your Mr Yankee to walk him to the privy. His bowels are unsettled, he said.'

'Father will have to do it. For all I know, Mr Winter has gone into town with Miss Armstrong. Perhaps they have eloped.'

Along, now, came Siam. Shuffling at the door.

'I think not. My laddio, *you* can attend Mr Darwin. Go to the parlour and see if he will come with you.'

'T'aint my place,' he said.

'Well, it certainly isn't mine!' snapped Mrs Brummidge. 'This house is in an uproar today. Go and offer some help. I've luncheon to get on the table.' She turned back to the oven and peered inside, batting against the steam and sniffing judiciously. 'Not one of my better efforts, but it'll have to do.' She turned. 'What are you waiting for, child? Do as I say.'

Still he did not move. He juggled his hands in his pockets.

'What do you have there?' said Mrs Brummidge, all glower. 'Pocketed something from the Master's vitrine, have you? Turn out your pocket, let me see, or I'll be sacked for theft. I won't find another position at my age, not like this one.'

Siam brought out a handful of treasures. Rather than hold them out in his open palm, he dropped them on the tabletop. Two stones from the riverbank. A bit of old conker shell, its auburn shine from last September all weathered to grey. A black ebony pawn from a chessboard.

'That *isn't* from the set in the parlour. Upon my word, I believe it is.' Mrs Brummidge turned pale. 'Mr Clowd's chess game is useless without all its pieces. As I've been told often enough and no mistake. You've no right to go sneaking about and lifting things from us. I don't care what your heathen background. You ought to know better by now. You're in *England*.' She pronounced that with especial force, as if every knee should bow. 'Miss Lydia, make him put it back, and bring him to apologize to the Master.'

'I only holded it,' said Siam. 'I warn't taking it.'

'You took it out of the house.'

'Didn't know I was going out. Anyhows, now it's back.'

Mrs Brummidge wouldn't discuss it further. 'Miss Lydia.' In that tone, the cook's word was law. She turned to withdraw the joint from the oven. 'Drawing room, young lady. Have him replace the object at once. Then to the parlour, where you will see that this fellow apologizes for his behaviour, and offers to help Mr Darwin, poor soul, with his cramps and ailments.'

Lydia had been docile, almost amused at seeing Siam upbraided. 'Come along,' she said. She led him up the steps and through the passage to the front of the house. Her father was in the parlour with Mr Darwin. The door across the corridor, the door to the drawing room, was closed. 'We don't even *come* in here any more,' she said. 'I can't think when you found the moment to steal around our house on your own. You might have opened any door and . . . found me unprepared for company.'

'When Mr Josiah took Mr Darwin out to visit the necessary. I just standing in the hallway. And your father, he crying or something. I coon't go back in there. So I look around in this room 'stead.' His hand on the doorknob.

'Very well. Go in again.'

He opened the door. The drawing room was still shaded with curtains. Outlines, dust, a faint odour evocative of Mama. It had been Mama's room primarily. They did not use this room now.

'Why they cloths up on the picture?'

'It's not a picture. It's a mirror,' said Lydia at the doorway, gasping in small silent intakes, keeping her voice level. 'A practice in this country to drape the mirrors when someone dies. It's outrageous that you've made me come into this place. Put back the piece now, I don't like to be here.'

'Who do,' he muttered.

'That's a rude thing to say as a guest, in this house, in this nation.'

'I'd leave iffen I could.'

'You may get your chance.' She felt light-headed and fiery. 'I'll tell your dallying Mr Winter, when and if he ever returns, that you've stolen from us. Perhaps he'll reconsider whether to keep on endorsing your *bid* for *freedom*.' She went further then, swayed into recklessness by the miasma of loss in this chamber. 'I do believe it may be the law of the land that thieves are deported. Certainly a fair number of felons have been marched to World's End and sent down under, never to return.'

'Down under.' He said it with the sound of an oracle, slow and horrified at what was emerging from his mouth. He set the pawn upon the chessboard so softly there was no little click of ebony upon marble tile square. None of the other ebony pieces, nor their ivory twins, shuddered or flinched. The world was dead.

'Down under,' she said again. 'Oh, what's the bother?' There was noise from the kitchen, a warm deep note, Mr Winter. He'd expected to meet up with Lydia again but she rejected him summarily, for his courtly attention to that stupid governess. He deserved whatever he got. 'There he is. I shall go and tell him at once of your perfidy. Wait here.'

She closed the door. He was alone in the dark, waiting.

Down under. Back home. What was the difference, what difference did it make? In a half hour, had he undone everything merciful that had happened to him in his otherwise merciless existence?

Who had he become, just by menacing this jittery white girl? He felt altered, other than himself. Nothing was like it had been before. *Am I even Siam?* he wondered. He had not always been Siam, he'd had another name. At Dover, the minister of customs had examined his papers and then asked a question in an accent too quaint for an American boy to understand. Mr Winter had given the tiniest nod of his head, so he'd murmured, 'Yes I am.' But the officer had heard 'Siam.' He'd written that down on the paper. Siam had had a ready-made alias he hadn't intended to choose.

The room was so dark. He felt gone, invisible, as if he had no more presence. All for a little black toy that had no face. He went past the chequered board on its table. He ventured to the mantelpiece and found a footstool by the hearth. He climbed up, and pushed aside the purple cloth that hung over the looking-glass.

The light was poor. Siam couldn't see himself at first.

'He's in the drawing room,' came Lydia's sharp voice in the passage. 'Go and say your piece, Mr Winter.'

A knock at the door. 'Are you in here?' Mr Winter's voice angry.

The boy might have answered 'Yes I am,' or 'Siam,' or even 'Samuel,' had he been in there. But the drape was settling across the looking-glass. The room was empty.

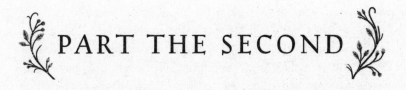

PART THE SECOND

There are bits and pieces of the Thames all over Oxford, runnels and reaches and backwaters – 'more in number than your eyelashes,' Keats said – and beneath the very centre of the city runs the Trill Mill stream, a gloomy underground waterway in which it was discovered, one day in the 1920s, a rotted Victorian punt with two Victorian skeletons in it.

– JAMES/JAN MORRIS, *OXFORD*, PAGE 31

CHAPTER 27

A noisy place and dark, the world has always seemed to Siam. A millstone working upon its quern not grain but shale, or glass, something splintery. The last light with any real warmth had been at home, long ago, in a place and a time that no longer existed, with people whose names he didn't say even inside his own mind. As if by thinking of them he might betray them anew. Might put them to some further punishment beyond that which had been accorded them by the slave-hunters.

Now, the boy is momentarily impressed by the silence. The drape on the other side hasn't fallen all the way back, it seems. An uncovered triangle of glass, hardly the size of his hand, remains. He climbs down onto a footstool placed in *this* room just where he had positioned it in the *other*. Curious. He is stealthy, a cat making no noise. The room is very like the one he has just left; equally dark, shrouded. It's too gloomy to know what sort of room it is. Possibly a second parlour. He hopes this isn't the room where Mrs Clowd is laid. He wouldn't want to be in a dark place with a spooky corpse.

He puts his hand to his face, palm side in because he knows the back of his hand is darker and will reflect less. Creeping up to the mantel and keeping as low as he can, he peers through his fingers across into the room from which he has escaped. Beyond the dark room with the chessboard, out in that passageway, a vector of summery light suddenly sluices, describing a wedge of golden swimming motes. Into the glare, struck as if by fire, Miss Lydia advances, and steps a foot into the dark other room. Her ghoulish pale hair falls upon her neck. Her hand lingers on the doorknob uncertainly. She opens her mouth and says something. Her expression betrays vexation, perhaps the start of worry. She may be calling his name, but he can't hear it.

In the absence of sound, he hears traces of things that he heard in a handful of hidey-holes from Georgia to Tennessee to Pennsylvania and other places. He and his party had learned to disappear in a split moment, sometimes stowed all together, sometimes separately. But he'd always been with one or the other of them, never alone. A smokehouse in the Blue Ridge steeps, a sugaring shed in Brooklyn. Smoke and sugar. And once in the gritty mouth of a coal mine, where they'd huddled in darkness, afraid to strike a match for fear of firedamp, that methane monster.

Disembodied words from the memory of those moments attach themselves to the soundless speaking of Lydia, who is addressing someone in the corridor behind her.

> *Don't know the names they'd be using, farmer; but when you got black rats in the woodpile no need to know their names before you trap them.*

> *If we find you're harbouring stolen property, we'd not be averse to burning this ham house down.*

> *Sending cargo up north, ma'am? Ma'am? Why, you look like you near swallowed a sack of saltpetre, ma'am. Not going to harm a whisker on your old chin, ma'am. Put down your gun, it's liable to make a row and waken the cooey-doves.*

Behind Lydia, into the room, comes Mr Josiah. Siam can't see his face clearly; Lydia is in the way, and so are the tears in Siam's eyes. He doesn't dare wipe them; the movement of his hand would attract attention. He squeezes his lids shut. Even through closed eyes he can sense when the light has gone out of that other room. When he cautiously looks about, he sees the light has largely disappeared from this room, too.

There is no telling when that missie will come back, hunting him. Siam doesn't want to plot an escape route in the bright sunshine of an Oxford noon. He'll hide here till tempers cool and his brains warm up. He has to think about what next. He hunches down to his haunches and makes his way forward, feeling the edges of tables. He brushes against the chess set. But that was in the room he just evacuated. Another set here, an identical one? Even in the anonymous dark, he can feel the forward pawn, just like the one he has just replaced. A little thing to bring him such trouble. It meant no harm – as if things could have meanings.

Oh, but now he's knocked it on the carpet, and can't make it out in the gloom. He leaves it be.

As much out of habit as not, he backs up into the open hearth, which is clean, clear of andirons and ashes. If someone opens the door, he'll be simply shadows, no more, the ghost of smoke.

In Cheapside last week, in London, he'd come across a chimney sweep at dusk, fresh from his day of labour. Boy or stunted man, bowed by a hawking cough, that person stared at Siam. Bright eyes alert in his sooty face. He'd said something to Siam. Blessing or curse, neither Siam nor Mr Josiah had known, for the fellow's mouth seemed thick with growths that made an already difficult accent into an impossible language. But though his words had been hooded, and the spit on the paving stones viscous and bloody, the sweep's eyes had looked full of pity and mercy. When he gathered up his brooms and his brushes and turned away, it seemed to Siam like losing another brother.

At this memory, Siam thinks he might climb the flue. He has

done this before, once, stealing through the big house with Clem the time he was loaned to pick the cotton fields of Bellefleur or Bellerive or Bellefuck or wherever it was. Clem had later been found out and beaten, but he'd never let on Siam was trespassing in there, too. Siam wonders if the chimneys here are made the same way, with protrusions for the hands to grasp. He'll find out.

He makes a start of it by feeling to make sure the space is wide enough for his head and his shoulders. He stands up, gingerly, into the darker dark. He raises his hands and gropes, and locates a hold. With one hand on the brick and the other pressed against the wall of the flue, he pulls himself up so his feet are not standing in the hearth any more. He wedges himself a few feet upward, angled in the flue like a twig in the neck of a brown glass bottle. But he can't find a second brick with which to pull himself higher. Then the first one breaks in his hand. With a mighty crash, he slips to the hearth. Somehow, against his plans and hopes, he smashes through the hearth, or maybe it opens on a hinge for the dumping of ashes into a cellar. He continues falling through the dark. Eventually I'll reach the kitchens and fetch up in a pot of stew, and ruin their lunch, he thinks, and almost begins to laugh, as if his despair has a bright aspect to it. Still he falls. The kitchen must be a long way down, he thinks, halfway to Hell.

CHAPTER 28

Lydia remarked, 'How curious of the child. Where has it gone?' She could hear her own voice taking a public, amused sound, as if Siam were a toddler scurrying under tabletops, and she were pretending ignorance of it, for his delight.

'Why would he come in here?' asked Mr Winter.

'I sent him to replace something he had' – Lydia hadn't clarified for herself just how far she was going to go with this – 'collected.' She glanced first at the chessboard. Her eyes hadn't adjusted to the gloom. She couldn't tell if all the pieces were there. 'He is playing a game on us.'

'He's not the type to play games. Siam, come forward, if you're here.'

Nothing stirred in the room. Lydia was confused. After these months, this terrible space still seemed the laying-out room, and would remain so until her father stirred the grief out of it. It wasn't her place to throw open the curtains. Yet she crossed to the windows and did just that, for the weasel child had got the better of her. 'I can't believe he's slipped out a window. Look, they are latched, each one.' She turned. The two dozen chess pieces stood in their proper ranks. 'Is he that stealthy that he might have slipped out behind my back? But it was scarcely turned.'

'You under-guess his capacity for intrigues.' Mr Winter took the room by eminent domain. He strode to check the shadowed side of the dresser, where the brown and white pieces had wakened and were winking dustily in the surprise light. The Staffordshire leech jar, its perforated lid set aside, held a clump of dead flowers set there in memoriam months ago. Brown stalks and curled petals. So little colour left that Lydia couldn't remember what sort of flowers they'd been. Rhoda must be frightened of this room, and avoided it since the occasion. What a failure of a maid she was. Lydia crossed the room. She twitched the violet drape into place around the over-mantel looking-glass. She smoothed the cloth.

'I asked him about his escapades,' she said. 'My, how he husbands his story. If you're the one who has trained him to hold his tongue, you've done your job well.'

'As a guardian, I can only reinforce lessons that his life has allowed him,' said Mr Winter. 'The boy has a history he would sooner forget. I know some of it, and I would let go of it if I could. Some realities are too onerous to be borne by nations, let alone by children. But we are all chained in this.' He sounded cross yet his words rolled out smoothly, as if he'd prepared his statement for a sympathetic congregation. How fond of his own sonorities, for a young man.

'Lydia, Mr Winter.' That was her father's voice beyond the door to the drawing room. 'I insist. Mr Darwin requires assistance at once.'

She was all daughter, that was all she was. 'Yes, Father, of course.'

She swept the American abolitionist out of the room. 'But this is not right at all,' said Mr Winter in a backstairs voice to Lydia. 'Siam is too petrified to go off on his own.'

'I shall find Siam playing with our Alice, no doubt. She's about somewhere. I shall make it my chief aim to locate them, right now. Oh, but isn't the day filled with missing children!' She spoke lightly and with a hushed voice. This focus, this emphasis required her to lean into Mr Winter's shoulder. She overbalanced, though. She had to catch herself on her fingertips against his broadcloth, an accident of poise. Her blood leaped in her arteries to counterweigh the advance.

The great man was in the passage, his broad famous hands flat upon his waistcoat, thumbs touching, little fingers pointing to the floorboards. She allowed herself to sense the presence of illness, intellectual temerity and theological scandal. He moved by in a froth of white whiskers. Fame and mystery, they are two sides of any earthbound prophet. There was a hint of sharp mustard in his wake. She pulled the door to the drawing room closed. She leaned against it, hands clasped behind her back. She watched Mr Winter grasp Darwin's elbow and lead him towards the side door and the privy.

'Lydia.'

She turned to look at her father, who raised an eyebrow. It was not her foray into the unused parlour that he was commenting on, but that she had been there with Mr Winter. Unchaperoned. 'Remember who you are,' he told her, before turning his face away.

Ah, but that was easier said than done, she thought. In order to remember who you are, you have to have known it in the first place.

Her father stood in the passage by the parlour door. He was distracted by both his colloquy with Darwin and his concern for Lydia. What he said next – she could hear it quite clearly – may have served two lines of thought at once.

He said gently,

> *'Genus holds species,*
> *Both are great or small.*
> *One genus highest, one not high at all.*
> *Each species has its differentia, too,*
> *This is not that, and He was never You.'*

He may have been talking about the Saviour. Or about Mr Winter. Or possibly about dinosaur relics in the Oxford Museum and great apes in the Congo basin.

'Shall I tell Mrs Brummidge to bring out the luncheon?'

He rubbed his face. This may have been a nod, or a grimace. He said, 'Alice is keeping herself quiet today, anyway.' He passed back into his parlour. He closed the door upon Lydia's caution and her anger.

In the kitchen, Mrs Brummidge said, 'So you've misplaced the visiting heathen creature, too?' She heaved the joint out of the oven and onto the butcher's board. It was blackened on one side like a log removed from the hearth. Mrs Brummidge chose some words unsuitable for Rhoda's ears and the maid went rash red. But Lydia refused to flinch at the assault, which barrelled on. 'For Lord's sakes! The young scamp must've scarpered up the front stairs whilst you was tossing your ribbons at his master. He's playing with Alice in some quiet way, and that's not right. Not in this house, with no Missus to remind you or Alice what's done or not to be done. Go up at once, and if they're around, bring them both down. I'll dish up some scraps and milk gravy when I've done sorting out the platters. Perhaps a dark boy will prefer the charred bits.'

Lydia flew up the stairs. The day seemed to be coming unstitched. It reminded her of her first and only trip to London on the railway. They'd crowded into a carriage with other passengers. Everyone, without considerations of privacy, talked their business across strangers. All their plans of what was doing in the City, and who was up from the country stopping in Lincoln's Inn Fields, and when someone would return, today or another, and alone or not. Lydia tried not to listen but her ears insisted. The railway carriage rocked, at the stupendous speed of quite a few miles in an hour, and the railway company didn't seem to care if someone dropped a ham on the floor, and which child had forgotten to use the loo, and whether Auntie Pretzel would remember to collect them in Paddington. On lolloped the carriage, as if time would work out all concerns eventually, with remorseless accuracy, no matter how the passengers barracked about their lives. Alice had sat and looked out the window at the rushing world, and she hadn't seemed to notice that she wasn't alone. Lydia noticed.

Lydia glanced in the nursery. She knew Alice wasn't there. Lydia could feel Alice in the house as one could feel a spirit or an intruder. But Lydia might be wrong about Siam. Who knew if he was readying to make off with something more valuable? That the Clowd family had little of value but what was broken among them didn't occur to Lydia. She sensed trickery and slippyness in Siam, as if he had evaporated in order to implicate her somehow. In something. She loathed him for it. She wanted to find him out at a greater crime, and cry foul.

Dinah the cat and her two kittens slept in a lazy, shedding heap upon a trunk in a sunny window. Lydia nearly pitched a shoe at them. It would have felt satisfactory to let a shoe go, but she didn't. She gritted her teeth and passed by, opening chamber doors and even wardrobes in case he was hiding therein.

He couldn't have climbed out upon the roof, surely? The window over the front portico was flung open, wide enough for a limber lad to scramble out, and woody vines around the trellis might have allowed him to climb down. But in the heat of June that window was always open.

She went up another half-flight to the box room under the eaves. This dusty space featured only one window. Union cloth was tacked across it. She ripped it down. The view from atop the house gave out over the heads of trees to the river and meadows. She might see Siam on the run. She could hurry downstairs with news for Mr Winter about his miscreant.

No boy to be seen; nor Alice; nor Ada; nor that pesky Miss

Armstrong. They had all been swallowed up in their own escapades. Ought Lydia start to be anxious for Alice? It wasn't unusual for the child to wander off, but this day was beginning to feature a comedy of absences. What Puck might be bewitching the neighbourhood with metamorphoses, parliaments, evaporations and misalliances?

She saw Mr Winter waiting a few feet off from the privy. He was studying the bees that hovered and swam over the snapdragons. She might have hallooed, if girls her age did that. She lifted her face in case he felt her gaze and saw her staring, so she might be caught looking statuesquely into the distance. The glassy summer noontime paused, trembled upon its long silent note of heat and anticipation. A few clouds over the Cotswolds cast upon that horizon a rich, regal grey, with a nap like Parisian velvet.

CHAPTER 29

The housemaid had pulled closed the drapes of the cloak of seaweed. The fronds interlaced and locked like iron mesh around Ada, the maid, and the performing troupe.

The seaweed, though dead and dry, was still growing. It seethed and twitched densely. Soon it had filled in all the spaces among the strands. With no horizon to settle her eyes upon, with little sense of up-and-down or here-and-there, Ada was unmoored. Blood pounded in her eyelids but devoid of the orangey pulse that happens when one closes one's eyes at the bright seaside. She seemed motionless, in an attitude like a figure in a tableau vivant intended to reprove. *The Virtues of Modesty, Restraint and Perspicacity at Play in Elysium.* Though struck with paralysis in the dark, she had the uncomfortable sense of velocity. As if she and her companions were moving at a remarkable speed, and unaware of it. As if they were ignorant, decorous creatures painted around the rim of a dinner plate that had been sent hurtling through the air towards someone's head.

Ada was not accustomed to thinking in such terms. Such aggressive equations.

But crash they did not, or not so they noticed. The housemaid opened a button to let in some air. Though some peculiar sounds caught Ada's attention, none of them seemed to be Jabberwockian, as she had come to think of it.

'I always find a change of clothes so brightens the mood,

don't YOU?' asked the housemaid as she released Ada into the daylight. The child fell out of confinement onto her knees, which hurt like the dickens. It took her a moment to straighten up and turn around. In her new agility she still favoured one leg.

She found herself on a gravel walk. But for the housemaid, Ada was alone. 'Where is this?'

'The path you find yourself upon,' answered the housemaid.

'What happened to the marionettes and to Humpty Dumpty?'

'Oh, they were wanted at the garden party. They were afraid of being late. Humpty Dumpty didn't want to be turned into a devil egg, which in the annals of kitchen science is the same thing as an angel egg. The Queen of Hearts has a robust temper, you see. And anger gives one an appetite. So her edible guests do try to keep her from losing her temper.'

'But I wanted to go there, too,' said Ada. 'I'm sure that's where my friend Alice will be. She is ever one for a party, especially if there are charades, or games and prizes.'

The housemaid had finished removing her seaweed robe. She was folding it into a small square, about the size of a pincushion. She popped it into her mouth. 'How unfortunate if it starts to rain at the party, as I've just eaten my weather apparel,' she said. 'Then again, seaweed gets so very wet in the rain.'

Her voice was different to how it had been. Ada realized that her young fresh face was now lined. She had turned pale. Her eyes blinked, rheumy and kind. She had shrunk, and her shoulders were hunched. She looked like the sort of aged matron who might be in charge of collecting tickets at a parish luncheon. 'You're not yourself,' said Ada.

'Travel tires one, don't you agree?' replied the old woman. 'So I've changed my clothes. It seems to go on forever, life. Still, when I get home, no doubt I'll feel sprightly again. Take my arm, dear, as I have trouble navigating over this treacherous gravel.'

'Where are we?' asked Ada, looking about.

'I have no idea. It seems perhaps to be a Zoological Plantation of some sort. I think we are the exhibit. Do you see the bars behind which we are caged?'

The old woman indicated a set of low hoops, like croquet wickets, set in the ground along the edges of the path. They formed an airy, imbricated fringe between well-kept lawns on either side.

Ada said, 'Those aren't the bars of a cage. They are fences meant to keep us from walking upon the grass.'

The old woman demurred. 'They are for our own protection. Otherwise, visitors who come to stare at our peculiarities would pluck us to shreds and turn us into decorative items for their homes. What type of specimen are you?'

'Begging your pardon, but I am no specimen.'

'Oh, you most certainly are. I believe you may be a fine example of a Rogue Child. No one seems to be hunting after *you* to fetch you from this durance vile,' said the old woman. 'As for me, I am a White Queen. Very rare in these parts. I frighten the natives. Quite often I frighten myself, but that is only for practice so I can do my job in the public *mêlée*.'

Ada knew she ought to be polite to a member of royalty. 'I believe travel has made you confused. This is simply a garden path. We could step over that low ridge of iron hoops and trespass upon the grass whenever we wanted.'

'Such ignorance in the young. If you think you are so free, try straying from your path. You should know the truth about captivity. Go ahead, my dear. Try.'

Ada went to the edge of the walk and began to step over. The lifelong stiffness that had been absent since her fall through the shaft now seemed to afflict her in the hip, however, and she couldn't raise her ankle more than a few inches. She turned to explain about her ailment to the White Queen, who smiled wincingly. Then the old woman directed her alabaster sceptre towards her own feet. Ada saw that the Queen's shoes were affixed to a dial of some sort, like a plaster stand.

'Why, you're a chess piece, more or less,' said Ada in amazement. 'No wonder you are having a hard time walking.'

'I glide but I do not jump. Shhhh, I believe we have company.' The White Queen cocked her head and rolled her eyes to one side meaningfully.

Along the grass on the other side of the hooped edging strolled a Lion, a Unicorn, and an elderly Sheep. The Sheep was trailing some undone knitting out of a carpetbag.

'Don't look now,' said the Unicorn, 'but the most revolting creatures are on display over there. Don't look. Don't.'

All three of them turned and rushed to the edge of the path and leaned over, making faces at Ada and the Queen.

'Just ambling along as if it owned the road. I call that cheek!' said the Lion.

The Sheep adjusted a pince-nez. 'I recognize a Queen when I see one in captivity. Would that all Queens met the same fate!' Her companions laughed halfheartedly but sent glances over their shoulders to make sure such sedition had not been overheard. 'But what in nature or out of it could that other revolting thing be?'

'It's a mere trifle, no less,' said the Lion. 'Either that or a plum pudding.'

'I never saw a plum pudding with such a foul expression on its face. I do believe it's not a comestible at all,' said the Unicorn. 'It's a mythical creature, I suspect. It doesn't exist. It's a child.'

'We saw a child just a little while ago,' the Lion reminded him. '*She* existed.'

'Ah, but where is she now?' The Unicorn shrugged. 'Imaginary, I tell you. A matter of legend and superstition with no basis in fact. So is this one. Swords and swordfish, but it's an ugly brute.'

'I am not,' said Ada.

'It thinks it's talking!' said the Sheep. 'Isn't that droll, isn't it queer! Hello, whiddle whillikums, how is your hawwible life today? Blah blah, it replies, as if it can understand us!'

'Was the mythical creature you saw called Alice?' asked Ada.

'It thinks it knows all about our lives. Did its owners give it a pamphlet to study before prodding it out of its Creature House to parade its ugliness before the paying public?' asked the Unicorn.

'I think it's rather dear,' said the Sheep. 'I should like to take it home and hang its head on the wall above my occasional table.'

'What is your occasional table when it occasionally is something else?' asked the White Queen politely, as if trying to change the subject from Ada to something less offensive.

'I choose not to recognize it when we pass in the street,' replied the Sheep. 'Sometimes it is an ornamental iron fawn in a dubious coiffure, sometimes a wheelbarrow putting on airs. I cut it severely.'

'I *like* that one,' said the Lion, pointing. 'Here, Queeny Queeny, if I point a stick at you will you snap at it with your little royal dentures?' He could see no stick at hand so he grabbed the Unicorn around the neck. With swiping motions he thrust the horn of his friend over the side of the path at Ada and the White Queen.

'I'll make a pudding of *you*,' said the White Queen. 'When I hang my crown up, I spend my leisure time as a housemaid, so I have learned many tricks of the kitchen, believe me! I'll thank you to mind your manners.'

'It's so real, yet so banal,' said the Sheep.

'Let go of my horn,' said the Unicorn. 'It's ticklish.'

'Did you fail to board the Ark? And did you drown?' Ada asked of the Unicorn. 'Did Noah even *try* to save you?'

'Rescue is a myth. Don't believe a word of it,' said the Unicorn.

'We mustn't linger,' said the Lion, releasing the Unicorn. 'Zoos are a form of happy diversion, but the light is lengthening. We ought to push on. I hope you still have the invitation to the party?' he asked the Sheep.

'Oh, dear, yes,' she said. 'I understand there is to be an execution.'

'What is to be executed?' asked the Lion.

'Manners and fine taste, amongst other things. Let's hurry along.'

'Tell Alice!' cried Ada. 'Tell Alice I am coming for her!'

'Aren't children so like real life?' said the Lion as they all opened up parasols and began to ascend in the breeze. 'And yet so *not,* too.'

'I still think it's a trifle,' said the Unicorn.

CHAPTER 30

It is an ordinary day in Oxford, just one midsummer day in the 1860s. The clock has struck one. Mrs Brummidge has finished laying out the luncheon. She has let her employer know the table is set. She has dumped the water used for boiling the pudding into the stones of the soakaway, and she has sat down in the shade outside the kitchen doorway. She is sucking on a horehound drop.

This story is spattering along on unregistered reaches of the edges of the famous town. The town hardly acknowledges the likes of Mrs Brummidge. For her part, Mrs Brummidge knows nothing, and will never know anything, about Charles Ryder and Sebastian Flyte and Zuleika Dobson, Harriet Vane and Lyra Belacqua and Jay Gatsby, George Smiley and James Bond, or even Captain Jas. Hook. They are yet to be imagined. In any case, Mrs Brummidge doesn't read fiction. She hasn't the patience for it.

It might be worth considering for a moment if the built landscape inspires in authors the invention of romantic individuals. Of course, architecture is impervious to rants, petitions, to shrieks of rape and the murder of martyrs and all the other human noise. But is one of the satisfactions of carved space — that is, massive stone laid just so — that it calls out for the creation of heightened characters to live up to it? Even if those outsize characters are ourselves, our own cleansed, resolved natures? The ancient Greeks may have thought so. (Drama was perhaps invented by the natural amphitheatre, and not the other way round.) The medieval masons of Chartres and Reims built windowed bluffs that laddered light into heaven; and peasants, in perceiving their own rights to salvation, began to imagine other rights, too. So Oxford, at its inception a huddle of theologians and divines, grew into a city of dreams, and much good may come of that. Little surprise that Middle-earth and Narnia were both discovered here.

Yet this story takes place outside of the most famous sites. No murder in the Sheldonian, no undergraduate lust in the reading room of the Radcliffe Camera, no academic intrigue in the Senior Common Room of Balliol, no capering over the leads of Christ Church, no spicy infidelities in the back passage at the Ashmolean, no spiritual remorse before William Holman Hunt's *The Light of the World*. Most of this story takes place on Oxford's margins, the area where the maps of famous buildings and renowned sites tend to pale and give out. The undifferentiated reaches marked *HC SVNT DRACONES*. Beyond the old town walls. You won't identify the exact mile of riverbank that ties together the lives of those in the Vicarage and the Croft. The river changes its course by grains of mud every day, imperceptibly. A rural district yields indifferently to development, plot by plot. And once the colleges open to women, fifteen, twenty-five years hence, the late-Victorian houses of Norham Gardens and the like, those anxiously fanciful, tall brick ships moored behind their garden gates up and down each lane, will obliterate this scrap of unsanctified north Oxford. It will remain only here, on these pages.

Perhaps we love our Oxford because it seems eternal, and we can return arm in arm; while our private childhoods are solitary, unique to each of us alone, and lost. We cannot point them out to one another. Only, sometimes, in the text of a book here and there, we tap the page with a finger and say, 'This is what my lost days were like. Something like this.' But even as we turn to the fellow in the bed beside us to say, 'Yes, this passage here,' whatever it is we recognized has already disguised itself, changed in that split instant. There is no hope that our companion can see what we, just for a moment, saw anew and hailed with a startled, glad heart. Literary pleasure, and a sense of recognition and identification, real though they are, burn off like alcohol in the flame of the next heated moment.

CHAPTER 31

So, yes, the luncheon is set, and the great man is brought to table. He is not sat at the foot, for that was Mrs Clowd's place and will never be used again. He is placed at Mr Clowd's right hand. Mr Josiah Winter sits at Mr Clowd's left. Rhoda brings forward the first course, a mock turtle soup. She retires to hover in the pantry. She listens to spoons clink upon porcelain. The men speak intermittently, affably, but without the race of competitive chatter Rhoda knows from meals at the boardinghouse in Jericho where on her off-days she sometimes shares a meal with her sister, who is in service to an addlepated old cleric hunkered down among the other rubbishy types there.

Rhoda has nothing to do with the disappearance of Alice. She has paid little attention to the child. The little girl, a bit of a pill. Rhoda pulls up Alice's bedding every morning and wonders at the doll left on the chest. Alice never sleeps with a doll as other girls might. Was she always this rigid, Rhoda wonders, or am I only seeing her as she is today, these months after the passing of her mother?

Alice? Eager to put every foot right, to live every moment correctly, to balance or redress that slashing crime perpetrated by an unfeeling universe? Or to forestall it happening again? Strange little Alice, playing in the penumbra of her father's moral consternation. She can't help but absorb some of the stress of that man's grief. Put plainly: if we aren't made of eternal stuff by a Creator who bent low upon the earth to fashion us, how can we hope for an eternal soul that might return to Him? And how can we hope for the promised reunion of souls when this created universe has run its course?

Of course Rhoda doesn't put Alice's situation like this. She thinks, scatteredly, Peculiar mite, that Alice. Whatever haze of apprehension attends the thought of the missing child is quickly dissipated. In the moments before the soup bowls must be removed – they dine *à la Russe*, in stages, unlike the hobbledehoyfreeforall service at the boardinghouses – Rhoda goes to soak the tea towels in an enamel basin. She studies her own cuticles. She has moved on from any further reflection about Alice's character.

Mrs Brummidge and Rhoda: these two people are here, too, in the story, along with the newborn Boy Boyce, that squalling infant, the presence of whom first sent his sister Ada hustling out of the Vicarage with a jar of marmalade. The dropsical Mrs Boyce, the distractible Vicar; they inhabit their own Oxfords. They don't realize that they might remember this day for the rest of their lives. The fatal day rarely announces itself, but comes disguised as midsummer.

Our private lives are like a colony of worlds expanding, contracting, breathing universal air into separate knowledges. Or like several packs of cards shuffled together by an expert anonymous hand, and dealt out in a random, amused or even hostile way.

CHAPTER 32

Lydia wasn't hungry. It was too hot, she thought. Still, Mrs Brummidge would report to Mr Clowd if Lydia neglected to eat anything. So she sat at the kitchen worktable with a hunk of bread and some cheese. She didn't care for soup, but Mrs Brummidge delivered a portion to her regardless. Lydia was put out at not having been invited to dine with the gentlemen, but in truth, Mr Darwin scared her a little. And Mr Winter probably would have ignored her over the joint and the peas, or been condescending. So perhaps it was best she stayed in the kitchen. With the residual heat of the oven, however, she felt dizzy and not entirely herself.

'We can't get rid of you, it seems,' said Mrs Brummidge in a here's-trouble voice. Lydia looked up. She wasn't surprised to see Miss Armstrong once more. That woman seemed yoked to this household today by a gum-rubber cord. She lowered her parasol and entered without invitation.

'I am on the edge of being alarmed.' In the absence of a gesture of welcome, she sat down.

'Only on the edge?' replied Lydia. 'Is there any way I can help . . . ?'

But the woman was calmer than she'd been earlier. Perhaps Mr Winter had soothed a few of her separate hysterias. She accepted a bowl of soup and dandled the spoon above it, preparing her strategic remarks before beginning her meal. It's the spoon of Damocles, thought Lydia.

'I went across the river. No luck. Then I returned to the Vicarage. Ada is still gone,' she said. 'I didn't make a fuss as there was another medical moment going on. I'm surprised *you* aren't more distressed at your sister's continued absence.'

'You don't know Alice very well.'

Lydia was glad Mrs Brummidge was collecting something from the larder, so missing this exchange; otherwise she'd have charged into this conversation. Lydia went on. 'Alice lives in a queer no-man's-land, Miss Armstrong, as far as we can tell. She isn't capable of malice and she hasn't discovered deviousness. No doubt you're wise to become exercised over the disappearance of Ada. But for this household to do the same over Alice's adventures would be ill-advised. Alice will return when she does. Likely, Ada will be with her. I think you are rather overwrought today.'

'It's hardly your place to say so,' snapped Miss Armstrong. Still, she was a guest here, and Lydia was as much as the Croft could boast in the way of a proper hostess, so Miss Armstrong scooped some soup as a gesture of closure. When she had swallowed the first mouthful she continued. 'Mr Winter waited with me while the boatman finished his lunch. Until Mr Winter felt he must return to attend Mr Darwin, I learned a great deal about the new work Darwin is considering.'

'I see,' said Lydia, who saw mostly that Miss Armstrong now seemed alert to the significance of Mr Darwin. But Lydia took little interest in questions of natural history. Mrs Brummidge, having returned to the kitchen, went about her business, ears cocked.

'At home in Kent, Mr Darwin showed Mr Winter a most peculiar orchid. It was sent to the great naturalist from an island off the coast of Africa. I forget which coast and which island. Geography is a sore mystery to me. In any event, the nectary of this amazing plant, according to Mr Winter, is an eleven-inch tube. Surely no insect flies around, even in darkest Africa, with an eleven-inch proboscis. Such would be ungainly. Yet Darwin imagines a moth possessed of a rolling proboscis, like an uncoiling snake, that could collect the nectar. Such a moth could retract his implement and propagate the species by visiting a sister plant. I don't think such a strategy is likely. But just imagine the mind that can imagine such a thing.'

'You are flushed with the effort of imagining it,' observed Mrs Brummidge.

'It's known as the Star of Bethlehem orchid,' said Miss Armstrong with complacency, as if biblical allusion must deter any unsavoury associations.

'And the insect would be a variety of the species *magi,* in that it comes bearing gifts,' said Lydia.

'Malarkey and confustication,' said Mrs Brummidge, trying not to laugh. 'Rhoda, pay no mind to nonsense.'

'I hate to pester you with questions,' said Lydia to Miss Armstrong, 'but when you were returning here from the Vicarage, I don't suppose you caught sight of Mr Winter's boy roaming about? He came back to the house with me but then scarpered off somewhere like a wagtail in the underbrush. Mr Winter went in to dine without knowing where the boy has gone. And I understand the guests intend to take the mid-afternoon train back to London so Mr Darwin can return to Down by nightfall. This is an arduous trip for a man with his set of conditions. Mr Winter won't be able to postpone their departure just because his boy has gone larking about.'

'I saw no sign of that child,' returned the governess, 'but when luncheon is over perhaps Mr Winter and I can make another perambulation together and look for *both* our charges.' She smiled at Lydia as if grateful the girl had scared Siam away. Oh no, you don't, thought Lydia. You're not making your jelly out of my jam.

'You people lose children the way scholars lose gloves,' declared Mrs Brummidge. 'Lydia, I've had enough of keeping my place. After luncheon you'll go and locate our Alice, and no chatter about it. Yes I know your casual confidence, but if only for my nerves. I can't take more of this, and I won't. My heart, you know.'

'They'll all be found together, no doubt, playing a childhood game, Ada and Alice and Siam. The soup is quite strong, Mrs Brummidge.' Miss Armstrong's anxiety over Ada had quite settled itself, Lydia noted.

'It's my belief his interest in that boy is unseemly,' said Mrs Brummidge. She wouldn't elaborate upon the matter. Shortly thereafter Lydia spilled her bowl of soup towards Miss Armstrong's lap. Her aim was poor. Hardly a dozen drops landed where they could do the most good.

CHAPTER 33

When Siam was able to believe that he had come unto another new world – as different from England as England had been from Gwinnett County, Georgia – he tried to take note of what this world was. A name would be helpful, like Little Egypt. Which was what the plantation had been called, the one from which he'd come out under pain and suffering, like the Israelites into the desert. Names of places mattered. Little Egypt. Bellerive. Down House, the home of that kind, distracted old man that Mr Josiah was courting. But if Siam could reckon no name for this place yet, he'd at least sort out a portfolio of impressions regarding what it was *like*.

He came to his senses, if these still were *his* senses, sprawled on his hands and knees in a patch of ferns. Falling through some sort of hearthside chute, he'd expected kitchens, a root-cellar, an ash-bin. Like any number of dank and spidery clinches in which he and Clem had been hidden. Or if he'd somehow been tipped outside the Croft, surely he'd be within sight of its narrow mullioned windows? But he found himself in a forest of some sort. Young trees with spindly trunks were established in sward smooth as felt, not thick with undergrowth like an American woods. As if woodland creatures cropped the grass here and kept it level.

He sat on his haunches. He rubbed the dirt and char from his face. With a little uncertainty, he stood up.

The tree trunks were regular, like slender columns of iron. The canopy above was brown with shadow. He saw no sign of sky. This forest was, in fact, as dark as the room into which he had climbed to escape – but he couldn't think of that person's name he was trying to avoid. The older girl with the blond – the blond whiskery business on top. Perhaps he had hit his head and he was still in that space? He wished he could walk to one side and push aside the – the hanging things that kept the light from coming in – coming in the glass – but he couldn't think of the name of the set of glass panes that let light in.

Must be shook up. That long fall. My words flown right out my head.

He turned around. In all directions the woods seemed to go on with sameness. It was impossible to tell which way to go in order to find his way back to—

What *was* his name, that rescuer, who had brought him all the way across the sink? No, not the sink . . . across the water, the big water?

A sound in the underbrush made Siam turn his head. A creature hurrying, pausing, sitting up, looking about, twitching its white whiskers, checking an item on a chain that came out of a pocket in its . . . cloth wrapping. The creature had funny ears covered with white fur, and a pouff of a tail. It said, 'If only I could remember how to tell time, I'd know if I was late or not.'

'I din't know time was something you could tell,' said Siam.

'One can tell time to hurry up, to slow down or to stop making such a dreadful racket,' replied the thing, hopping a few feet closer and examining Siam with a placid expression. 'One can tell time to be still. Two can tell it the same thing, only more forcibly, with the courage that comes from uniting voices in song. However, I seem to have forgotten how to tell it a thing, including to be sure to wipe its feet when it comes in from tramping about at all hours.'

'Does time have feet?'

'You've heard of time dragging. What do you suppose it is dragging, its nose? Of course it drags its feet.'

'I din't know it lugged itself about. I thought time flew.'

'Ah, yes. The wings of time.' At this the creature swung the object about on its chain and then let it go. It soared upwards but didn't return. It had become lodged. 'It's stuck on that protrusion,' observed the creature. 'I feel I should know what that is called, that lengthy thing with greenery clinging to its tips. Can you hear the tick-talk, tick-talk, that time is telling us?'

Siam listened carefully. Yes, just barely, he could make out a regular pulse from the dial at the end of the chain. 'So time does fly,' he said. 'Does it fly back, too?'

'Oh, yes. Remember the poem. "But at my back I always hear / Time's wingèd hat-rack hurrying near." It's a bother to have a wingèd hat-rack always poking one in the back, but there's little else to be done if time is to return. Is that a hat-rack it is stuck upon, do you suppose?'

'This has a name,' said Siam. He shook the trunk to see if he could jostle the moments loose. 'Still, I can't remember if it is a hat-rack or not.' His labours were useful. The time-machine fell off. The creature caught it in a furry paw, and slipped it into a convenient slit in the cloth that was bracketing its middle.

'Shall we stroll together for a spell,' asked the creature, 'now that we have the time?'

Siam couldn't think why not. He was twice the size of this woodland animal. He might easily outrun it if it called the authorities. 'You headed anywheres special?' he asked.

'Oh, very special indeed. Though I can't recall what it is called. Perhaps you might suggest a few special sites? I will choose from among them which is the nearest.'

'Perhaps you are headed to . . .' Siam scratched his head. 'To a shoemaker?'

The creature looked down at its unshod hindquarters. 'Uncommonly rude of you to point out that sartorial impossibility for one of my appendages, not to mention the other one.'

'Maybe you are headed to a headache factory?'

'That sounds peculiarly right, and yet: *no*. Any other ideas?'

Siam tried to think of wonderful destinations. He could envision a fireside at night, and massive warm presences that gave off gusts of affection and protection. He could find no words for that sensation, though. 'You hunting for a velveteen ladle? A hill conquered by a rocking chair?'

'You speak reams of nonsense. I don't understand a word you say.' While they had been talking, and scratching their heads out of consternation, the path had meandered through some thickets of red berries and prickly leaves. At the other side of this growth the forest suddenly tapered off. They came out into a spill of sensible light.

'My goodness,' said Siam. 'You a White Rabbit, and you can speak.'

'And you're a black child,' said the White Rabbit. 'I don't suppose we're twins who have lost our way in the Wood of No Names?'

'Is that where we were?'

The White Rabbit turned about and pointed. 'Yes. And we've lost time in there, I'll warrant.'

'No, we din't,' said Siam, 'it's in the pocket of your waistcoat.' For suddenly he remembered *pocket* and *waistcoat*.

'Oh, my,' said the White Rabbit, examining the watch and snapping its lid shut, 'this will never do! I'm late for the *garden party*! She'll have my head, see if she doesn't!' At this, the White Rabbit tore off across the meadow, as if the hounds of a hunting party were on the scent and baying for blood. Siam remembered what that was like. In three shakes of its tail, the White Rabbit was out of sight.

I won't go backwards, thought Siam, for I know little enough about where I am as it is. A forest that makes you forget the names of things is a dangerous place to hide. Odd that no one ever mentioned that animals could talk here. Perhaps that's why Mr Winter was so eager to speak with Mr Darwin. Evolution a mighty power, could it yield up creatures capable of argument.

Then again, thought Siam, what good did arguing ever do me?

He tried not to be alarmed. After all, the past few years had brought him dozens of surprises, many of them unpleasant, and yet here he was. But where *was* he?

Siam had a fine memory. He pictured the page of the book that a kindly New England matron had opened upon a table. She had picked up his hand and run it across the letters. She'd made him say the words that the letters were spelling. She had thought she was teaching him to read, but she was really only feeding his memory bucket, slowly and carefully. He moved his hand in the air before himself. He felt the words in their kinky, obstinate shapes. He said their sounds aloud:

The Pilgrim's Progress,
from This World to That Which Is to Come;
Delivered under the Similitude of a Dream.

That he could carry such a memory still, even after he'd spent some time in the Wood of No Names, gave him a boost of courage not unlike a draught of ale. He straightened up his spine and went forwards, whistling.

CHAPTER 34

Lydia decided to sabotage Miss Armstrong's plan of waylaying Mr Winter for another private walk. Lydia said, 'Since Mrs Brummidge insists I find Alice, I'll go and look, and return with Alice *and* Siam. Mr Winter will be *so* pleased.'

'I'll have your head for a doorstop if you don't bring Alice in,' swore Mrs Brummidge. 'I'd go hunt her myself did we not have Mr Himself to dine.'

'I'll come with you, Lydia,' said Miss Armstrong promptly, as Lydia had gambled she would. Better Lydia should suffer the company of this sycophant than that the governess should prey upon Mr Winter while Lydia was out of doors. Miss Armstrong continued. 'Before the men finish their meal, let us put this hide-and-seek routine to an end. Those children are having us as fools, I fear. It is the age-old gambit of the young against the adults. No doubt you played it in your time. I am certain I did.'

Lydia couldn't decide if she had ever engaged in such a campaign, and if so, whether or not she had finished. She was only aware of confusions, which might be the same thing. Resenting Mr Winter and his chivalry towards the governess, resenting Miss Armstrong's menacing solicitude about him. Lydia was also aware of a throb of guilt about Siam's hiding from her. Still, wherever Siam might be, it was his fault, not hers. *She* hadn't pocketed a game piece. And from a room more mausoleum than anything else. Lydia found herself becoming indignant all over again.

It's not easy to be half of anything. Half-adult/half-child is a state with no reliable signposts.

She left her soup half uneaten. She ignored the brown slices on the bread tray. She rose from the table. 'If Siam isn't found soon, do you suppose Mr Winter will send Mr Darwin home on his own? So the American can stay here to search for his lost boy?'

'I believe Mr Darwin's needs take precedence.' Miss Armstrong's air of propriety about Mr Winter's obligations, thought Lydia, was nothing short of insolent. 'Mr Winter told me that the old scholar hasn't left his home in months. People come to him. Whenever he *does* venture up to London, he lets no one know, or he'd be bedevilled with invitations. Your father must be a very honoured friend of Mr Darwin's for the man to travel so. He is feeling the stress of this trip. Nothing would induce Mr Winter to abandon him. Mr Winter has his own petition to make of Mr Darwin, you see.'

'The gentleman went around the world on the *Beagle,* and it took five bloody years,' intoned Mrs Brummidge. 'If he can't get from Oxford to London on his own, he needs to grow a new pair of flippers.' She made vaguely *arfing* noises under her breath for the next several minutes.

Lydia and Miss Armstrong went to the garden. Love-in-a-mist, sweet sultan, bachelor's buttons. Hardy annuals. 'The children are *not* in the house,' said Lydia. 'I am sure of this. It's true, Alice can be silent as a corpse when she is in one of her dream games. I found her once lying under the bed staring up at the mattress ticking. I sensed her presence, there's no other word for it. She'd been there all day.'

'Which room?' asked Miss Armstrong.

'Does it matter?'

'Perhaps not.'

In fact, the bed in question had been the bed that Mama had died in. Lydia had yanked Alice out by her elbow and by the hem of her skirt. Lydia had had to slap Alice, twice, to make her blink her eyes and notice where she was.

But though one child, an Alice-like child, could pretend to marble, three together would give themselves away in whispers and giggles. The children must be underfoot, hiding somewhere obvious. It was a matter of thinking where to look. Of becoming like unto a child again. Of yielding to that paradox: that the least powerful among us are privileged with the greatest exposure to feeling. The greatest susceptibility to impression.

'When Ada has come to visit before, the children have played in the garden,' said Miss Armstrong, looking about. 'Shall we leave no stone unturned?'

'They won't be under a stone,' said Lydia.

The property of the Croft consisted of a small orchard (four trees), a kitchen garden with a hen run, and a misshapen apron of grass across which Dinah sometimes stalked with stiff swivelling legs, and her kittens pounced, black and white against the green. The garden had been Mrs Clowd's domain. Much flourished now that ought not to do: stands of weed, frotheries of vine that had not been cut back in the appropriate season. No shortage of blinds for hide-and-seek. In ten minutes Lydia and Miss Armstrong had made a thorough circuit, even peering into the chicken house. No stowaways could be found.

'We've *been* back and forth across the river path and the nearer meadows,' complained Miss Armstrong. 'Does Alice often go far afield on her own?' She spoke with a minimum of disapproval, for which Lydia was grateful.

'Not very far. She's too young.'

'We all grow up.' This, a bulletin from the front, courtesy of the five or six years Miss Armstrong could claim against Lydia. Lydia despised her all over again. 'On my way here after checking at the Vicarage, I called out to the Trillings' gardener, who was passing by in a rowboat. He hadn't seen the girls. I didn't ask him about Siam, but I suspect he'd have mentioned if he'd seen a displaced child of that variety. Are you *quite* certain the children aren't hiding in the Croft? You've examined all its crannies and particulars? You've been to the attics? Have you remembered the basements?'

'I've been all about, but not to the cellar,' said Lydia. 'It is too wet to keep anything there but spiders. In any case Pater minds the keys. No, Alice is not at home, Miss Armstrong; I've said that already. And I insist she wouldn't venture into town. She's given to silence and solitary play. She doesn't seek out company. She avoids it generally. And in among the colleges and the market there is nothing *but* company. Even in the long vac, when the streets are quieter than in term, there'd be too much fuss made over her.'

'I can't see that Alice deserves much fuss.'

'She's become a motherless child, Miss Armstrong. That type of creature calls forth a response from all, whether Alice requires it or not. Though she abhors the stickiness of sentiment. She's too brave for that.'

'Then there's nothing for it; Alice and Ada must have put their wicked heads together and decided to strike out further afield along the riverside than we've thought. If we find them, we'll find Siam in tow, I hope. He'll have caught up with them. They've had a good start and might have gone a distance. Shall we push on beyond the University Parks? It gives us something to do, anyway, while the men are finishing their meal.'

Miss Armstrong plunged forwards across the fields to the river path. She was a land-borne ship in full sail, the large violet and ivory oblongs upon her plaid skirting a semaphore of maidenly distress. The fabric billowed and luffed about her. Lydia had to grip her own skirts in her fists and run to keep up.

When they'd settled to a more sensible pace along the path, heading south, the governess said, 'I've always approved of Ada's friendship with Alice. Ada Boyce is frail and speculative where Alice is decisive. I fret for what life will deliver unto poor Ada, with that distortion in her skeletal structure.'

'It has never seemed all that dreadful to me,' said Lydia.

'The appliances that she wears perform adequately. But no one will have a young woman with a stoop and a gimp. No one respectable. I think it quite fine of Alice to overlook Ada's short-comings so nobly.' She glared this way and that, tendentiously. 'We all have our shortcomings, it seems, though some are less visible than others.'

About Miss Armstrong's opinions of Lydia's shortcomings, Lydia didn't enquire. They fell into a silence more companionable than either of them expected. Something about the lull of the long noontime pulled them along the riverbank without further negotiation. They angled along Longwall Street and crossed the High. At the Botanic Gardens Lydia lunged in and peered, walked until she had seen the whole outlay and listened for give-away sounds of laughter, and then returned. The two of them then kept a brisk pace into Christ Church Meadow. Only when a bell sounded again marking some quarter hour – Lydia had lost track of where in the day they were – only then did they pull up and reconsider. Were they going to walk all the way to London?

'I suppose we must start back,' said Miss Armstrong. 'But despite your protestations about Alice's meekness, let us go out to St Aldate's and return through town. Perhaps the girls have emboldened each other to venture in that direction. Oh, Ada will get a good thrashing from her father if he ever catches wind of such impertinence! And *your* father will have to reconsider what is to be done about Alice. A convent school in France, perhaps.'

Lydia was about to say that she herself was perfectly competent to tend to Alice, but then she'd been the one to lose sight of her. So, meekly, Lydia allowed herself to be pulled along towards the bulk of Christ Church College, hulking as it did beyond the meadows like a great stone creature in repose, possibly in senescence.

As they neared the back of it, they saw a door swung ajar in a high garden wall. 'Do you think the girls might have ventured there?' asked Lydia.

'The colleges are not open to children, and most especially not to girl children.'

'Alice is not one to notice prohibitions even when they're posted. We may as well have a quick look.' Before Miss Armstrong could squawk, Lydia darted forward. She put her head into a small pretty cloister of a space, the sort where an afternoon garden party with croquet and lemonade might be held. Foxgloves and larkspur poked and swayed in abundance. A serene male sort of calm obtained. Then Lydia saw a fellow in a corner by a ground-floor window. Its lower sash was flung up. He was patting a contraption of some sort as if to tame it. He was looking at his pocket-watch with some distress. He caught sight of Lydia. He said, 'Oh, heaven provides! Miss, M-miss, might I ask you to perform m-me a small favour?'

'You may not go in there, Miss Lydia,' said Miss Armstrong, reaching the door in the wall.

'It's between t-t-terms and no one is about, and only for a m-moment,' said the man. He was a student or a young fellow of some sort, agitated and twitchy. He made an arabesque in the air next to his equipment, which on closer inspection seemed to be a camera on legs. 'I was set up to take a p-portrait, you see, and my companion m-must be detained. And the light is . . .' He mumbled. Had he said 'delightful'?

'We were looking for my sister,' said Lydia, cordially enough.

'Come, whi-which of you? – It is to be a self-p-portrait, only I cannot release the shutter. H-he was to do it and I cannot say where he has disappeared to.'

'Half the world has gone missing today,' said Miss Armstrong. She entered the garden as if stepping into a tepid footbath, gingerly.

'Show me,' said Lydia.

The young man beckoned to the black fabric arranged on an armature of wires. A portable cloth cave set up in the middle of midsummer luxuriance. 'Miss Lydia, you don't dare,' said Miss Armstrong, but she was not Lydia's governess. Lydia did indeed dare. She ducked into the black tent with the stammering student. It was warm and close. The mechanics of the camera looked faintly menacing, as if intended for the use of a surgeon.

'You just look here, you see. I will call out when I am ready. You must press this b-button all the way down, and stay qu-quite still and do not jostle the delicate thing. All will-will – well, it just will,' he concluded. Lydia followed the instructions well enough. There was nothing thrilling about being in close quarters with him. He had all the electrical excitement of a suit of clothes upon a dressmaker's armature. She had somehow hoped for more.

There he went, out of the black envelope and across the lawn to the half-opened window. He perched himself against the frame, his buttocks slightly elevated on the stone sill, one leg gently uplifted. He might have been climbing into the window, or just perhaps leaving. In the square in which she peered, he looked tentative. Sweetly alert, and trembling. If he was after an expression of sobriety and scholarship, he was well wide of the mark. He looked as if he had just been slapped and perhaps had felt a rush of confused pleasure in the aftershock.

'If you w-would be so kind,' he said, 'just now.'

Huddled under the black cape, the misbegotten midnight, she

saw him in the aperture, and pressed the button. A click and a whirr, and time seemed to stand still. He froze in his place, bland innocence masquerading as a young man. Perhaps into the room behind him someone had opened a door, for an imprecise glow briefly backlit a corner of the otherwise black glass. Against such correct rectitude it took the look of a hastening creature not intended to be caught by such a tool. The blur of a swift Siamese cat, perhaps, or an Angora rabbit.

CHAPTER 35

Lydia waited. He was caught now, but unless he stayed still for a full minute the effect would be compromised. She wasn't to budge an inch for fear of jostling the box. The black tent was, for a moment, a shroud. She wondered if, for the dead, the life they had left behind seemed to them frozen the way this young scholar was frozen. The dead could no longer intervene, regardless of the need. But they could study, perhaps, the frozen past from which they'd been exiled. Look at the creases of the skin beside his eyes, the hesitant light in his face. Look at the creases in circumstance. Press up against everything that has happened exactly the way it had. Reconsider how forces actually work, and how one thing leads to another, until it is frozen, and all that is left is the intelligence of it, but not the living nub.

'Highly irregular,' said Miss Armstrong, when they were done. The scholar stammered and apologized and was grateful. 'The colleges are not arranged so that young women might be entrapped in the garden,' said Miss Armstrong ferociously. She turned on the young man as if she thought he must be lying when he said he had not seen Ada or Alice or Siam. Then all at once it occurred to her that she, too, was trespassing upon precincts forbidden her. She pulled Lydia away.

Along St Aldate's, Miss Armstrong pressed Lydia on what it

had been like to be cloistered in the dark with that student, as if there was a secret to be learned about huddling under a cloth with a young man. Lydia demurred.

CHAPTER 36

The White Queen and Ada continued along the path. They couldn't step sideways, for the lawn edging prevented them from straying. Neither could they retreat, for when they looked back, they saw that the gravel path had retracted and formed a little loop like the eye of a needle. Should they bother to retrace their steps, they'd only be marching forward again in a moment.

Ada was perturbed. 'Let's *try* to reverse ourselves—'

'Hard to do that without a looking-glass,' interrupted the White Queen. 'And why bother?'

'Because,' Ada continued, 'as far as we can see, this path only goes forwards across the meadows, while the Sheep and the Lion and the Unicorn flew off in the opposite direction. They were going to the garden party, back that way, and we will be wanting to get there before long.'

'*You* may want that,' said the White Queen. '*I* want peace among all nations. Either that or a lemon drop, I can't decide.' Still, she fed her arm through Ada's. They began to traipse along the return path, which curved neatly to join up with where they'd been. The exercise had taken a quarter of a minute, but it had been so much fun, or so little trouble, that they started out again along the loop. The White Queen said, 'Who is this Alice about whom you keep chattering about who is the girl about whom you keep mentioning?'

'Everyone knows Alice, it seems,' said Ada. 'She's been all through these parts. Yet we're having *such* a time catching up with her.'

'I don't know the girl of whom you refer, referring that is to the girl about whom you keep referring. Whom I don't know.'

'Do you feel quite all right? Is this making you dizzy?' Ada asked the White Queen as they began their fourth circuit. 'We could stop if you like. There's no need to continue.'

'To whom much is given, much is expected of those to whom much is given,' replied the White Queen uncertainly. 'I expect.'

'You're talking in circles,' said Ada. 'Let's go on.'

But the path seemed to have so enjoyed their company that it now limited itself to no more than this single loop around a small hummock of grass. There was no backwards or forwards, no horizon of past or future, just a circle around.

'We *are* in a zoo,' said Ada. 'Look, we're caged in a pen, with the open world all around us, a temptation and a paradise, but forbidden.'

'No, that's the zoo.' The White Queen pointed. 'That enclosed circle of grass, around which we are now tottering around, and around, and around which we round with nearly tottering competence with which we totter around.' She looked ill.

Ada patted her alabaster elbow. 'You hush now and save your breath. We may be on this road quite some time. I shall tell you about Alice, since you asked. She is a friend of mine. Well, in actual fact she is my only friend.'

'Why — is that why is that? Why?'

'I have not been lucky in my limbs,' said Ada. 'They are not frisky enough. I frighten the other little girls. They run away.'

'Who who who who who who?' The White Queen's eyes were wide and dreadful, filled with terror either at the collapse of her power of speech or at the thought that Ada scared little children.

'Everyone except Alice,' said Ada. At once the thought of sensible, stoic Alice filled her heart and her breast to bursting. How queer that inscrutable child was. How beloved of so many. For the first time since slipping into the hole in the riverbank, Ada felt alarmed. *Would* she be stuck in this wonderland for ever, always chasing after Alice, never catching up? And *was* Alice all right? Ada began to cry. She was well-bred enough to know that crying was undignified. She tried to hide it from the White Queen, but the old creature noticed.

'Now, then,' said the White Queen with great effort. 'Now, then, now, then, now, then. There, there. There there there there there. Now, then now, then now. Now.' Though her face was rigid with stress, the White Queen leaned down. She creaked out a crooked smile. The old potentate was carved of ivory crazed all over with *craquelure*. Her expression, a rictus of caring concern, might have seemed a caricature of senile dementia. But Ada responded with brave gratitude. At least in her regard for a young companion, the White Queen is like Miss Armstrong Headstrong, she thought. If not half so highly strung.

'It's all right,' Ada managed. 'Alice, you see, is the reason I am here.'

'Hear, hear,' said the White Queen, or maybe that was 'Here, here.'

'She's the only one who – who—' Ada didn't know if she was stuttering from sudden emotion or if they had been around the loop so often that she was going loopy, too. 'Who—'

'Who,' said a voice that was not Ada's or the White Queen's.

The girl and the White Queen looked up. The mound around which they'd been walking had turned into a mushroom, and upon this spongy fungus lounged a Caterpillar, one distinguished by a vigorous ugliness. 'Who,' said the Caterpillar, 'are you?'

'Well, that's easy enough to answer, now that you ask it, and it's high time somebody did,' jabbered the White Queen. She hopped up and down with joy, relieved of her verbal paralysis. The white pedestal upon which she stood made impressions in the gravel. 'I am the White Queen, of course, any fool can see that—'

'I am no fool,' replied the Caterpillar, 'and so it follows that *I* cannot see any such thing. You a White Queen? You appear to be a migrating finial afflicted by a poor conversational technique. In any case I wasn't speaking to you. I was addressing the slug-like child at your side. Who,' he said again, drawing out the syllable like an elocution master, 'are *you*?'

'Well, I'm Ada Boyce, if you please,' said Ada, 'and I hate to rush matters along, but—'

'And if I don't please?' asked the Caterpillar, puffing upon a pipe of Oriental workmanship. 'Who are you then?'

'I'm still Ada,' said the child. 'Whether I please you or not, I'm still Ada. Even if you run away from me like some I know, I'm still Ada.'

'Caterpillars seldom run,' he replied loftily, 'unless pressed by the clamour of a devoted public. You were asking after Alice?'

'Well, I hadn't done that yet,' said Ada.

'You said to rush matters along, so I am anticipating. If you would like to ask *before* Alice, you are too late. She has come and gone.'

'Was she quite all right?' asked her friend.

'It seemed to me she had some growing up to do,' replied the Caterpillar. 'Or some growing down. I can't remember. Memory is unreliable, anyway.'

The White Queen said, 'I have a fine memory myself. I can remember when I licked an envelope to seal it. The envelope stuck to my tongue. I had to walk the envelope all the way to the Queen of Hearts myself. I was replying affirmatively to her kind invitation.'

'Her kind invitation?' asked the creature. 'What kind of invitation?'

'A garden party, as it happens.'

'And that is where Alice is going,' said the Caterpillar. 'Perhaps she has already arrived and been sentenced to death. If you want to catch the fun, I shouldn't linger here. In fact, I want to see the proceedings, and *I* shouldn't linger here. And I shan't.' At this, he turned into a butterfly. Ada hadn't known butterflies could manage to be so ugly. The Caterpillar lifted from the mushroom cap like an angel of death off an ottoman. It whisked itself away with a speed and a sense of destination hitherto unknown to its species. Just as it disappeared, it called, 'Don't eat the mushroom. You don't know if it is poisonous!'

'Do *you* know?' called the White Queen, but the insect had disappeared.

'Look,' said Ada, 'the garden path has vanished. We're free.'

'It's dangerous to stray from the garden path, they say, but when the garden path itself takes to straying, that's horticultural mutiny,' replied the White Queen. 'Look, bits of this mushroom have teeth marks in them. It can't be poisonous or the ground would be littered with corpses.' She reached up and broke off two pieces the size of dinner plates just as a voice cried out in alarm. It was neither the Caterpillar's voice nor the Sheep's, nor, in fact, was it much like any other of the peculiar characters Ada had met so far. The girl turned.

A boy came stumbling out of the woods. He waved his arms to dissuade them. He looked like the boy in the Sunday lesson book, from the page about Afric's pagan interior. 'Might do you harm,' he panted. 'A mushroom that virile. Best take no chances.'

'Who,' said Ada, imitating the vowels of the departed Caterpillar, 'are you?'

'You sound a big old hoot owl,' he said. 'I'm Siam, I am.'

'I'm Ada,' she replied. She turned to introduce the White

Queen. But it was too late. The White Queen had taken a mouthful of mushroom. She had frozen into a statue of herself. At least her expression looked pleased, as if her last meal had met with her approval.

CHAPTER 37

The shadow of Tom Tower had retracted from St Aldate's. It was concentrated solely upon the cool tunnel of Tom Gate below it. The doors stood open as if, in a grand parade, scouts were about to march through with buckets and brooms, six dozen strong. Through the blue tunnel could be seen a fountain and a still, green lake of lawn. Various distracted dons and a few gentlemen wafted about as if by the strengthening breeze, apparently so lost in labyrinths of their own scholastic minds as not to have noticed that Trinity term had already concluded. Otherwise the streets were emptying. 'Does it seem that a storm is coming?' asked Miss Armstrong.

'I wouldn't know.'

'Whatever might the time be?' One of Oxford's unhurried bells rang the half hour obligingly, but of which hour was it the half? The city seemed to have become unmoored. 'Did you know that at night Great Tom rings five minutes later than the hour in London? Oxford being that degree west of Greenwich?'

'Does that mean that at night it takes longer to get from London to Oxford than it does to get from Oxford to London? Or shorter?'

'Oxford is the beginning and the end of all nonsense. Don't be foolish,' said Miss Armstrong. 'I don't know what it means, I'm just jabbering.' On they pressed, towards Cornmarket. In the heat, the Saturday morning market was already disbanding. The streets were emptying as luncheons were being laid, cheese slapped upon the boards, shutters going up for an afternoon break and perhaps a slumber in the back room or a little something nicer if the wife felt overheated enough to remove her skirts. A dog padded across the junction at Carfax with all the insouciance of a gypsy tinker at the gates of a bishop's palace.

They turned into the Broad. In the light and dust the street looked as if lined by buildings made from skilfully carved oat bread. The spirits of Miss Armstrong and Lydia Clowd lifted at the sight of two girls emerging from Blackwell's, but those girls started to run away. 'Oh, Ada could never lift her limbs like that,' said Miss Armstrong. She slackened the pace that had quickened in hope. An older woman, a grandmother sort, next emerged from the shop. Her squawkeries were lost in the breeze. The girls paid no heed. They rushed on, laughing merrily.

Miss Armstrong and Lydia Clowd pushed east. The colleges, barricaded against the two females in favour of faith and reason, stood stolid in the strengthening wind. A squidge of something got into Miss Armstrong's eye, or so she said. She dabbed at her face with a cloth. Lydia turned to examine the reddening eye with a gallows mercy. 'A bit of grit, a midge, a fly, a plank, a mote, what does it matter?' Miss Armstrong snapped at Lydia.

'Whatever it is, blink quickly to flush it out, for if I'm not mistaken—'

Lydia was not mistaken. The Vicar was bearing down upon them from across the Broad. He was heading in the same direction they were, but faster. Miss Armstrong flinched. 'Reverend Boyce, sir,' she began as they seemed about to collide upon the pavement.

'You're far afield, Miss Armstrong, but I daren't stop to pass the time. The doctor has sent me to collect a new bromide suitable for the infant. We expected you back to help when you'd collected Miss Ada from the Croft. Have you given yourself leave for a perambulation? It won't do, Miss Armstrong! And in this heat! Watch out, weather's coming. Or, forgive me, perhaps you are on an errand for Mrs Boyce, did she send you out for—?' The Vicar caught himself in time. Family secrets stayed within the household. He pivoted. 'Good day to *you*, Miss Lydia. I hope you and your family are keeping as well as can be expected in this season of sorrow.' He didn't pause to see if his hopes were being met; he cannonaded away. The various demands of Mrs Boyce and the Baby Boykin got the better of him. Apparently he didn't know that his clumsy Ada was lumbering about God's good creation without the benefit of a chaperone. Lydia elected not to summon him back to clarify. For this she received a wordless moue of gratitude from the beleaguered governess. In a moment the Vicar had disappeared beyond where the Broad became Holywell.

In a low voice, Miss Armstrong said, 'Oh, what are we failing to consider, Miss Lydia? Where can they *be*? If they are lost, I am lost, too. I shall never get a position supervising children again. I shall have to go below-stairs.'

'How sad for you,' said Lydia. 'And of course, *they* may be dead. That's even more below-stairs than household staff.'

'You are cruel and then you are kind and then you are cruel beyond compare. I do not understand you, but there is no time to try. I ought to have told the Vicar. But he sends me into such a tizzy. He doesn't know the half of it!'

'Which half does he know? That you are incompetent, or that you are sentimentally excitable? Or is there a third half buried in there somewhere that even I can't detect?'

'Who taught you to bruit words about like a barrister? It is unnatural and unbecoming in any female. In a girl of your slender years it is demonic.' Was that a spatter of rain, or drops from a mop shook out an upper window? 'I do not put my heart onto a table in the operating theatre so that a young *voyeuse* like you can dissect it and see how it works or fails to thrive.'

Lydia fell silent. Not wanting to follow the Vicar, they took an alternative route, and turned into the Parks Road. Before long the University Museum gathered its stone haunches in the distance and grew larger as they approached. 'If you are let go, you could get a job dusting the bones of the great lizards dug up in the desert. Dinosaurs,' said Lydia. 'Those creatures are already dead, so you could do them no harm.' But perhaps she had only thought those words, as Miss Armstrong did not rise to her own defence. Lydia tried again. 'Did you ever see that claw of a dodo, and the painting some Dutch master made of it?'

'The Vicar does not approve of his household visiting such a place. It only strengthens the temptation to doubt. I understand the painting is famously vile, in any case. Such a creature deserves to be extinct.'

'Were ugliness the criterion for extinction, we'd be freed of a great many matrons stopping to call and to console my father. Dodos, the lot of them.'

On they passed, across the University Parks, towards the Cherwell, towards home, past Park Town, where the university's dons, forbidden marriage, were said to lodge their female companions. Once or twice Lydia thought she saw the hastening figure of the Vicar emerging from the plunging shadows of an elm, becoming faint in the light. But from this distance that could be anyone hurrying home before the storm.

Were a dark boy standing in those shadows, thought Lydia, we might not even see him.

Then through the lane this time, hoping that the lagging girls and the stray boy might have turned up under their own authorities. But Lydia knew how everyone lingered under a death sentence. Postponing it with prayers and promises was as ineffectual as pleading upon a star, or throwing a copper into a wishing well. You lost your copper as well as your faith in wishes, and prayers.

CHAPTER 38

'Siam,' said Ada. 'What sort of a name is that?'

'It is like Lazarus,' said the boy.

'Biblical?' asked Ada. Not for nothing was her father a Vicar. Siam didn't reply.

Ada didn't understand Siam's point. Had he been put in a grave, like Lazarus? Or raised up from one? 'I always wondered if Lazarus *wanted* to be raised up from the grave,' said Ada. 'He had two sisters who were always arguing over whether to sit and listen to the Saviour or whether to do the washing up. Martha and Mary, do you know about them? I always think there must have been a third sister, perhaps named Maggie, who didn't want to join either of her sisters in their worthy tasks, but preferred to get dressed up and go out dancing like a Jezebel. The noise in that house must have been ferocious. The sleep of the dead must have some advantage, don't you think?'

'Where are we at?'

Ada had been so accustomed to the peculiarity of her day that it took Siam's question to remind her of her circumstances. 'I wonder. It's a very strange land, wherever we have strayed to. I assume you've just arrived, or you wouldn't be asking.'

'We came by London,' he said, 'but so gritty and foul. Not like here.'

'Are you alone?'

'Now I am,' he said. Then he corrected himself. 'Now I'm not.'

They looked about themselves. The White Queen seemed to be made of salt. She was blunting and softening in the wind. A bit of salt made itself at home in Ada's eye. She had to blink. She liked the White Queen quite the best among all the denizens of this place, but the poor creature was eroding fast. Now she was like a spool and now like a spindle. Now she was a pile of white sand tracked in from a foreign strand. As the miniature dune changed shape in rising winds, shrank to a mere pile as from a broken hourglass, something like a scrap of palmetto leaf revealed itself.

'Why,' said Ada, 'I do believe I know what that is.' She leaned down and plucked the item out of the salty sand or sandy salt. She shook it out.

'This is a cloak made of seaweed,' she told Siam. 'Come, let us try it on together.'

'That's not permitted of me,' he replied.

'Everyone else always makes the rules,' she said. 'Just now, no one else is here. Come in.' She slipped the seaweed over her shoulders. 'It's a capacious cape, with room for all. I have known it to be useful.'

'It smells like the air from Boston Harbor to Portsmouth,' he said, ducking under. 'It smells like all beginnings.'

As Ada began to draw the cloak closed over their heads, she looked about to see how the world had changed, for surely it had. It always did. She noted a perforated set of images coming through the cape. Glowing and insubstantial, as if thrown by a magic lantern, or several magic lanterns operating at once. She saw the mouse with the marmalade jar, and the great hall with the glass-topped table. She saw the seashore and the scraping roses. She saw the tired old Knight and the singing pig and the looping gravel walk and the troupe of liberated marionettes. The difficulty was in assembling such contrary information into coherence. Whenever she thought she might have begun to manage it, the images slid and shifted. The material meant something different. How very like a dream this all is, she finally said. Just like the song, merrily merrily, and so on. Like a boat on the Cherwell out for a summer picnic, and the Thames, and seeing what went past, and making up a tale that connected it all, while past it slid past it slid past. And life was just a dream.

Then darkness.

CHAPTER 39

Lydia and Miss Armstrong came onto the property of the Croft through the shortcut. The lone cow in her corner looked ruminatively at them, but offered no testimony about whom she may have seen pass, and in which direction. The main walkway led to the portico, though a path forked off around the side of the house. Lydia intended to lead Miss Armstrong that way, through the kitchen garden to the back door. Another spontaneous encounter between Mr Winter and Miss Armstrong would only make Lydia feel more sour in herself, and unsettled. But the front door stood wide open. Voices were heard in the steep midday shadows within. The choice was taken from her.

Mrs Brummidge was wringing her hands and wiping her eyes. Oh, no, they've been found, and it isn't good, thought Lydia. A sunk boat on the Isis, a rotting beam in some hayloft hideaway . . . The instinct towards panic, once experienced, cannot be unlearned. 'What is it, Mrs Brummidge?'

'It's the bloody Begum of Banbury Cross, that's what it is. I'm set to get what for, and no mistake,' said Mrs Brummidge.

'Whatever—?' Before Lydia could speak further, voices rose in the hall behind the cook.

'This is intolerable.' Pater sounded pained. 'Madame, I must insist that you take your leave at once.'

A volley of musical syllables flew forwards from the hallway.

A woman's accented voice, an oboe descant originating in the mysterious flyspecked Raj. Cajoling, syrupy. She appeared at the door hauling a straw hamper of some sort. A veil of blue and gold angled across her brow. From beneath a respectable tartan shawl cascaded several contrapuntal swags of glorious and unreasonable skirting. The woman was slim though more full of figure than most of the good wives and maiden aunts that Lydia had ever met. And dark, dark of complexion, though in a different way from Siam – dark persimmon – and glamorous beyond contemplation. But she was a nuisance, clearly. Mr Winter was obligingly seeing her out.

'The great man, his interest in the wide world, it must include my shells from the sea; it will finish his work,' she was claiming, as near as Lydia could hope to understand.

'Mr Darwin is in no condition to entertain impromptu guests. He came here under promise of privacy,' explained Mr Winter. 'You've been misinformed, Miss Gurleen. Miss Mittal. Madame Gurleen Mittal, whatever is proper to call you, Mr Darwin has no wherewithal to examine your collection.'

'She's here to show more than her seashells,' said Mrs Brummidge, brazenly. 'I ought never to have opened the door to her. Off with you, milady, and tell your brother he has overstepped, gossiping like that.' She waved the exotic woman down the walk with a flap of her apron. Gurleen Mittal disappeared at an uneven gait, her parcel of seashells bumping against her thigh. The bland English air in the garden was, momentarily, stained with incense of sandalwood.

'*What* was all that about?' asked Miss Armstrong as Pater appeared beside Mr Winter.

'It's my fault, sir,' said Mrs Brummidge, addressing both the gentlemen. 'I made a misstep. I only barely hinted at the name of today's guest, you see, to my sister, in service in the buttery at Balliol, don't you know. She may have chirped it to someone who chirped it to someone else. And Miss Mittal has a brother stopping at Balliol over the summer months to do research in maths and suchlike. But I had no idea the hussy would hear of this. Any excuse, and there she is at the door again. Setting her ribbons to charm the widower. This time I take the blame.' She lowered her head as if she fully expected to be struck, though Mr Clowd would not strike the top of a table.

'She's been here before? Those people, they don't know their manners.' Miss Armstrong fairly flashed outrage.

'They don't know *our* manners,' corrected Pater quietly. 'She may think she's doing a kindly thing for me, to appear with a basket of specimens and hope to lift the burden of conversation off my shoulders. I wish I'd never stepped up to help her brother find his materials in the Bodleian. But no matter now. She's gone. It's a mercy she didn't come earlier or our esteemed guest would have found us lacking in honour as well as hospitality. Mrs Brummidge, we *did* promise him anonymity.'

'Curse the day the Lord put a tongue in my mouth,' mumbled the cook.

'Mr Darwin requires to visit the facilities again before we set out,' said Mr Winter soothingly. 'Mr Clowd, would you kindly call for the carriage while I see to his needs? He's decided to stay in London tonight after all. He's too wrung out to get all the way to Down House in one day. Miss Lydia, Miss Armstrong, summon the boy, if you would. It is nearly time to go.'

Lydia opened her mouth, but no words came out.

Miss Armstrong spoke to Mr Winter's back as he headed inside. 'If Siam hasn't returned, then we have no earthly idea where he is. The boy has fled this house and its surrounds.' But Mr Winter, hurrying down the passage, didn't catch her remark, what with his concern for Mr Darwin.

'The young lad will be with Alice, no doubt,' said Pater, peering along the lane with an expression that suggested he was afraid Miss Gurleen Mittal might be huddled in the hedges, ready to pounce. 'Lydia, where is Alice?'

'Off with Ada,' Lydia said, she hoped. She hadn't the heart to say more.

'Oh, Mr Clowd,' said Miss Armstrong. She swept upon the portico and caught his arm. 'To be pestered by well-meaning townspeople of every stripe, common and exotic. Let us see your guests to their carriage without alarming them, if possible. Then, dear Mr Clowd, I fear we shall have to send for the constable.'

CHAPTER 40

The darkness in which Ada and Siam had stood was both close and echoing. There had been time, a lot of time, in which to characterize it, but Ada hadn't been inclined to sort out the wool from the warmth of it. A sort of sleepiness had come over her, a balmy complacency. It hadn't been so bad.

None of this occurred to her, really, until the husk of seaweed fell away from them. My, what was that, was really all she managed to think, before the insistent demands of *here* and *now* barked in her direction once again.

Siam was blinking in the light. Ada thought it was daylight, but then she realized that ever since she'd tumbled into the foyer of the rabbit warren, she'd found herself in a place with a light that was, somehow, not expressly sunlight. Shadows on the ground positioned what she was looking at, but they were insincere, sloppy things. They tended to wobble if she looked at them through the sides of her eyes. As if they were trying to get away with something. The sky was blue, but vapidly, evenly so. It didn't seem to thin at the edges or deepen at the apex. I wonder, thought Ada, if people ever see the overland sun in their dreams. *I* don't believe I've noticed the actual sun once since my descent.

'Where are we?' asked the boy.

'Well, a bit of here and there, it seems,' said Ada. They were standing on a square lawn that had been recently rolled in very even stripes, back and forth. It resembled a chessboard with lighter and darker squares. A thin and undernourished sort of woods grew up to the edges on three sides. Off centre upon the lawn loomed that same old pedestal table with a glass top. And upon the tabletop was a key.

Where there was a key there must be a keyhole, thought Ada. Turning around, she realized that the fourth side of the forest-room was a high stone wall in the uneven colours of scones and fresh farm eggs. The wall had a familiar look, as if it might edge a cloistered walk or a Fellows' garden in Oxford. A painted door that could use some touching up was set directly in the wall. 'I have a strange feeling I've seen this door before,' said Ada.

'I never,' said Siam. He picked up the seaweed cloak. He began to fold it up. When it was the size of a Cornish pasty he handed it to Ada. She didn't want to eat it.

And to put it in her pinafore pocket might look like stealing. So she slipped it in the heel of her left shoe. It wedged there without complaint.

'A keyhole,' he said. 'In the door. But I don't see no key.'

'There's a key on the table,' said Ada, 'though this is a table for a dreadfully lofty member of society.'

'We never do climb that mast.' Siam put his hands on his hips and leaned far back. 'It's a forbidding sky.' He meant the glass tabletop.

It is, thought Ada. As she looked, it seemed that reflections of something else steered and slid across the top surface. There was movement up there, soundless alarum of some sort represented in pale flickering shapes. But there was no way to tell what it might pretend to mean.

'The key, up there,' he said, pointing.

'I see it. Will it work in this door, do you think?'

'I known some keys and their habits.' He cocked his head towards the door. Through it, sounds of merriment and abandon. It was the brightest garden party of the season. It was where everyone would be. Ada guessed that she hadn't been invited because of her deformity. But maybe, now that she was not alone, Siam might find a way in. He was clever.

For a while they took turns peering through the keyhole at a festive affair neither could quite bring into focus. Ada thought she spied a recumbent Cat floating through the air, though perhaps that was a superior cloud in a feline formation. Then she imagined she saw Alice, at last, but a buxom grandee in a tortured headdress swept up and grabbed the child by the arm and concealed her from view. What Siam saw, when it was his turn, Ada could not say, for he didn't tell her.

'We want in there.' He said it neutrally. Perhaps he meant it as a question.

'I *do*,' Ada replied. 'I've been searching for my friend Alice since I got here, and everyone says she was inclining towards a garden party. Have you been looking for anyone?' she continued, remembering her manners just in time.

'No one to look for,' he mumbled. 'No one left.'

Ada had a hard time being sure what he meant. 'If they didn't leave, then they must be here,' she said encouragingly. 'Maybe in there.'

'Won't be. So it don't matter none. But we get in if you want to.' He looked at the key. Because the glass was invisible, the key appeared to float in the sky. 'Can't climb that big old table but I do maybe break the glass.' He hunted around for something to throw. He found a few small white rocks. When he tossed them they turned into blackbirds and flew over the garden wall. 'Contrary stones,' he said.

'How about your boot?'

He took it off. He pitched it as hard as he could. It banged against the underside of the glass tabletop, quite hard. The key danced, making a sound like tin thunder. The glass was resolute. The shoe fell down. It hit Siam on the head.

'Must be something to use. Some stone or other thing to throw. Nothing's unbreakable,' he told her. He went about on his hands and knees feeling in the grass. 'Hell's doorbell, what's this?'

'Show me.'

He opened up his hand. It was a small black game piece, perhaps from a chess set. 'Let me see,' she said, looking at it more closely. Then she said, 'Siam. What happened to your hands?'

He pocketed the item and put his hands behind his back. She said, 'Show me. Tell me.' He did not want to do that.

She would not let it go. Finally he opened his palms again. The skin on the inside of his hands was paler than the rest of him, a private sort of colour one might keep to one's self, for it looked vulnerable to Ada. But that was not what she needed to see. There were round marks on his hand, red and raw, all the same size, some of them overlapping. Each one about the circumference of a grape.

The sounds of the party on the other side of the wall may have carried on and they may have gone away; she was no longer listening. There was a terrible feeling in her insides. 'I want to know,' she said.

He relented at last. 'Back when we was all together still, they play a game one night. They planning to take us upcountry for loaning to another overseer, for the otherly cotton was ready and they needed hands. They'd some liquor the night before we was to leave.' She reached out and held his hands. 'It nothing worth saying now.' After a long pause: 'So, they tell us young ones iffen we want to buy our freedom, come on here. I din't like it but—' Another pause. '—but our own said, Maybe this your chance, it only gets worser when you get on in years. Maybe they knowed what going to happen to them somehow. Maybe they could see into days ahead. I put myself up for freedom. The bosses say it cost a dollar and I says I ain't had money paid me afore. We give it to you, they go. You collect a hunderd pennies in one minute by Master's timepiece and you bought yourself free. Then they shakes a jar of coppers onto the belly of a shovel and holds it over the campfire long time. When they think it fun enough, they say, get yourself ready, and now you go, boy. The pennies go in the dirt around the fire and I got to pick them up and keep hold on them.'

'Oh,' said Ada, with a sound like a kind of punch in the air, or out of it.

'I gets forty-two hot cents before that minute up,' he said, holding out his hands again. 'Here's the proof.'

'Oh,' she said. 'And no freedom.'

'Nothing next, but that we left,' he said. 'One by one, and not on the same path, turns out.'

'And here you are.'

'And wherever this be, I don't know. Some mystery or t'other.'

She lifted her shoulders and dropped them. 'Well. With me I suppose.'

CHAPTER 41

They heard an intrusion of thunder. They looked at the glass sky but the key above it lay there undisturbed. The indeterminate shapes above, those hints of a separate reality, scudded and shifted shapes, none of them nameable. Ada said, 'I know that noise, it's been following me. They called it the Jabberwock I think.'

'I know that noise, too,' said Siam. His face was grey as paste. 'We got to get us into that garden and hide us-selves there.' He went up to the door and felt it. A metal plate, in very small letters, said

KEEP OUT.

'Not too friendly,' he said.

'All doors say that, when they're closed,' said Ada. 'An advertisement to go away. But so what?'

'Use the key,' said the Cat, appearing at the top of the wall. It was flicking its tail dangerously, like a civet cat.

'We can't reach.' Ada pointed to the glass tabletop. 'Can you get it for us?'

'Cats do favours for no one,' it replied. 'Not to mention that it's the wrong key for right now.'

'Somehow that does not startle me,' said Ada. 'Little that has happened today has proven advantageous.'

'Try your pockets,' suggested the Cat, beginning to fade in the air, like wood-smoke.

'I have nothing left. I've given away the marmalade already.'

'Maybe I gots something,' said Siam, and dug his scarred hands therein. He came up with that characterless figure on a pediment, nicely turned in ebony. 'I took it,' said Siam, 'but I gave it back.'

'Maybe it *wants* to be lost,' said Ada. 'Is this a key in any way, do you think?' She turned to raise an eyebrow at the Cat, but it was gone.

Siam put it up to the keyhole, which seemed now to be little more than a bung hole. The head of the figure fitted neatly in the aperture. They heard no click, turned no knob. Regardless, the door in the garden wall swung inwards.

They walked through, hand in hand, and the air instantly seemed warmer, though still there was no sun to speak of, only a bland differentiation in colour and shadow upon the flowering borders. 'Well,' said someone, 'I never thought to see you here. I didn't think you properly brought up. Walking about on your own, no chaperone, like an urchin.' It took Ada a moment to realize that the nearby rose-tree was addressing her.

'Rosa Rugosa,' said Ada. 'You survived being transplanted.'

'Few do,' said Rosa Rugosa, 'but I always had a desire to grace the court. So here I am, doing my bit for beauty.'

'You look lovely.'

'They wanted to paint me white but I objected,' said Rosa Rugosa. She gave Siam a glance. 'I make no further comment.'

'There's a great deal going on here,' said Ada. 'Have you seen a girl called Alice?'

'I wouldn't say. I don't interview the madding throng. Though every type and token seems to be invited. The Queen of Hearts has a wide circle of admirers.'

'They look abject,' said Ada, scanning the bewildering assortment of guests.

'Well, the Queen is hot-tempered, and is constantly sentencing them to death. It tends to cast a pall on the chitchat. There she is now.'

From around a stand of violet larkspur came a ferocious-looking creature cut along the lines of a Queen printed upon a playing card. 'It is time for the entertainment, and where has that troupe of barmpots got to? You!' she barked at Ada and Siam. 'Are you the marionettes? Tie your strings on and get to work.'

'Begging your pardon, Your Highness, we are not,' said Ada. She didn't expect to be able to manage a curtsey but perhaps the seaweed inserted in the heel of her shoe gave her a rare balance. She dipped and swayed and returned without falling over, or even threatening to do so.

'Hmmmmpph. I don't recall your names on the guest list. I don't recall your names at all, come to think of it. Who are you? Where is the Master of the Household? Why am I shouting? Heed!' she bellowed.

'I'm Ada, and this is Siam,' said Ada.

The White Rabbit scurried forward and adjusted his spectacles. He carried a long trailing scroll of paper in which many holes had been cut. 'Your Highness,' he said. 'At your service.'

'Check the guest list, and tell me if Ada and Siam are upon it.'

The White Rabbit peered with grave intent. After a few moments he said, 'Ah, yes. Here they are.'

'Well, take them off,' she said. At this the White Rabbit pulled a pair of sewing scissors from a pocket and made two little holes. The paper scraps went into another pocket, which was stuffed with earlier excisions.

'You're not to be found on the guest list,' said the Queen of Hearts darkly. 'I have half a mind to take off your heads, now I've eliminated your names, but I need to work up to it.'

'If you please, Your Loudness, we're looking for a little girl named Alice,' said Ada.

'The place is crawling with objectionable creatures,' came the reply. 'I'm sure you'll find something nasty to take home as a door prize.' She reached out and plucked Rosa Rugosa with her bare hands. Ada caught sight of the rose's startled horror. Whatever had suffused her with character faded. She was no more than a limp crown of petals upon a torn stem. 'Here, this can be Alice. Now you can go.'

Before Ada could speak again, in another part of the garden a tawdry and hysterical brass fanfare sounded. It seemed to be summoning guests to the theatricale, as the Queen of Hearts was rushed away on the arm of the White Rabbit.

'My,' said Ada, laying the dead rose upon the peaty moss. 'Life is a very cheap thing here.'

'Cheap and dear all at once,' said the Rose from her grave. 'That's the thing. You'll figure it out sooner or later.'

CHAPTER 42

Mr Clowd looked at his elder daughter and then at the cowering Miss Armstrong. 'Whatever can you mean?'

'The children have run off, all of them,' said Miss Armstrong. 'Our Ada, and your Alice, and Mr Winter's Siam. They are having a pretend adventure and have forgotten the time, perhaps. Or they are in some sort of distress. We've been searching for them.'

'Lydia, how can this be? I thought you were looking after Alice?'

'Papa, you know our Alice.' Lydia made a dismissive wave of her hand, pretending an insouciance she didn't feel. 'All hours are the same to her. No doubt she's bullied the other children into going along on one of her games. I only worry about Siam, for Mr Winter seems about to depart.'

'We can't alarm Mr Darwin. He's been upset enough by the incursion of that uninvited Hindoo lady.'

'Oh, for shame.' Miss Armstrong was sympathy itself. 'I'll tell Mr Winter what is happening. Leave it to me, Mr Clowd.'

'But you were to be watching Alice,' said Mr Clowd to Lydia, weakly.

'She slips in and out of sight,' replied Lydia, in her own defence. A poor choice of words, perhaps. Mr Clowd turned pale. But even moments of dread are interrupted by creaking dailiness. A noise in the road, and Alfred was drawing up with the carriage.

Mr Darwin was emerging from the Croft and plopping a wide-awake upon his head. Mr Winter held his elbow as the intrepid naturalist steadied himself in the portico. Mrs Brummidge and Rhoda hung back in the shadows, an honour guard of domestic sentinels observing the passage of the great man.

'We'll get to the station ahead of the rain, I'll warrant,' said Alfred, tipping his hat.

'It wouldn't rain today,' said Mr Darwin without glancing upwards. 'It wouldn't have the nerve. Mr Clowd: I regret not having seen your other daughter, but the young have escapades of their own. My own little Annie, before she died at the age of ten, was always in a state of ambition and espionage. The comings and goings! Hold on to her, Mr Clowd.' He bowed to include Lydia. 'Hold on to them both. In time you'll find children the greatest comfort you can imagine. Indeed, they prove to be the only possible distraction from the unanswerable question of *why.*'

'You have been too good,' said Mr Clowd, miserably.

'Not good enough to answer your question of *why.* Each must await his cataphany in his own turn and time. In any case, no one can be too good; and I have merely returned sympathy to a sympathetic soul. Good day, my dear Mr Clowd.'

'We are shy of Siam. Call him forward,' said Mr Winter.

'I haven't found him,' said Lydia. 'It's as simple as that. He wasn't upstairs nor down, nor about the water-meadows. We went as far as Carfax and the Broad.'

Mr Winter's brow contorted; he blinked in disbelief. But Mr Darwin was hobbling with evident distress. He was minding his feet upon the paving stones and wheezing a pulmonary étude in a minor key. He needed his young friend's assistance. He seemed not to notice the consternation stirred up on the walk behind him, though Mr Winter kept turning his head at Lydia.

'What can you have done with him?' hissed Mr Winter, *sotto voce.* 'He's been glued to me since we left Rowes Wharf in Boston Harbor.'

'Here we are then, sir,' said Alfred, taking over and assisting Mr Darwin.

As Mr Clowd presided upon the step of the Croft and the staff peeped from the shadows, Mr Winter turned back to Lydia. He wore the look of a hawk at hunt. He frightened her. But now Miss Armstrong, of all unlikely barristers, came to Lydia's defence. 'Your Siam has come unstuck,' she said coolly. 'Perhaps in the presence of real children, he's remembered how to play.'

Lydia was emboldened to add, 'I wonder if the cost of your saving him from menace was the denying of his other liberties.' A tone of accusation rose in the way she slapped her words in place. She found her regard for Mr Winter turning to something like suspicion – though notice how often we lower suspicion upon others to avoid putting ourselves under scrutiny.

Now Miss Armstrong grabbed at Lydia's arm and linked it with her own. 'There is no need to fret, Mr Winter. See to Mr Darwin as far as he needs, all the way to Down House however long it takes. Return to Oxford tomorrow or the next day. The boy is larking about with the girls, no doubt. He can wait at the Vicarage with the Boyces till you return.'

'Nonsense, not with the new infant wreaking havoc in that family,' said Mr Clowd affably. 'Siam can stop here. Mr Winter, I agree with Miss Armstrong. She talks good sense. From what you've said, the child hasn't had a childlike day in most of his life. Let him roam and see what freedom means in England. No one will accost him. He'll turn up with our Alice and with Ada Boyce. We'll tell him he's to wait with us until you return for him. He can trust us.'

Mr Winter managed only, 'Siam is not adept at trust.'

'We'll woo him with our confidence. Or we will force him.' Miss Armstrong gave a brittle smile. She squeezed Lydia's arm cheerily. The girl hadn't asked Miss Armstrong to step forward, but she wasn't unhappy for the unforeseen alliance. She stared beyond the trembling Mr Winter at Mr Darwin, now settled in the carriage and leaning forward to see what the delay was. The white beard captivated her. He was like an image of the Ancient of Days.

'We're off then,' said Alfred from up top. Mr Winter had no choice but to depart.

Miss Armstrong dropped Lydia's arm the moment the carriage had cleared the property wall. 'And now it is time to call upon the constable,' she said. 'Mr Clowd, will we go together?'

'Midsummer evenings are long. I'm certain the children have merely lost track of time,' replied Lydia's father. 'Surely we have another hour before we need to become concerned. Alice will come home when the shadows lengthen at last. Would you care to take refuge from the sun, Miss Armstrong? The good Mrs Brummidge could fix us a pot of tea.'

Lydia followed them. Her grip on the moment was uncertain. She was demoted to a mute member of this noxious tableau. She was a sallow adolescent girl, no more than that. Her thoughts were seized within her, words carved immemorially upon an upright grey tablet. *Miss Armstrong has already given up on Ada. Miss Armstrong apprehends that her tenure at the Boyce household is done. Miss Armstrong is tendering a kindly attention to my father.*

CHAPTER 43

Ada thought, It's as if a botanical display and an athletics contest and a gypsy circus have all set themselves up in a hippodrome of some sort. Creatures and things bobbed and weaved this way and that, like cottage farmers and housewives on market day. If there were a central commotion amidst the sideshow specimens, it came from beyond a tall stand of ornamental rushes. The entertainment, perhaps, accompanied by hasty ragged music and cheers. 'I think since we don't see Alice on the lawns, she's joined the throng to watch the marionettes,' said Ada. 'Let us make our way there.'

'That Queenie told us we wasn't invited,' replied Siam, though he didn't seem perturbed by that.

'It's too varied a crowd for us to be noticed. We'll skulk,' said Ada. 'I've never skulked before, as it requires a talent for slinking and sloping. But I'm up to trying it now.'

'I can learn you skulking. Let's go.'

A hooded figure meandered by. He was made out of papier-mâché, coloured all over with dark paint, with a prominent jawline and protuberant eyes. He was studying a pamphlet. 'Pardon me, has the spectacle begun, then?' asked Ada.

'It's begun, and then some,' replied the character. 'The programme seems to be a very good one today.' He took a bite of it and chewed carefully. 'I do approve. A nicely varied offering, with body, heft, character and nuance. I believe they are almost up to the trial. I don't have any lines, but I'm trying to digest the proceedings before I'm called to do my work.'

'What work is that?'

'Why, I'm the executioner, of course.'

'And what do you execute?' asked Ada politely. But he had begun to run a bone-like finger along the margins. He was no longer listening. He veered away from them. He got his papier-mâché axe caught in the low branches of a hornbeam tree.

'I suppose I'm late,' said another voice behind them. 'The baby was such a pig today.'

Ada turned to see a fiercely ugly old woman tottering along in a headdress of stupendous proportions. It split in two as if it meant to disguise disfiguring horns growing out of her head. 'You don't know where they're all gathering, do you?' she growled at them.

'If you're looking for the marionettes,' said Ada, 'I suspect they're over there behind the sedge-grass.'

'I'm looking for the trial. I believe I'm wanted as a witness.'

'Who is on trial?' asked Ada.

'The marionettes will be if they don't perform up to snuff. Though I couldn't be bothered about who is the defendant. I'm trying to stay out of court. Aren't you dreadfully nosy for a little girl. Then again, it seems a day for it. It'll end in tears, see if it doesn't.'

'I thought you said you were wanted as a witness?'

'What made you think that?'

'You just said so.'

The wizened old creature frowned. 'Yes, they wanted me, but I didn't want *them*. A Duchess has better things to do than make a spectacle of herself.'

'Off with her head!' bellowed the voice of the Queen of Hearts.

'Oh, my, I hope they're not talking about Alice,' said Ada. 'We must hurry.'

'Do you know Alice?' said the Duchess. 'She was by my house earlier today. A right proper pill she is, too.'

'She's not,' said Ada.

'She is so. She taught the baby to scream.'

'A baby knows how to scream all by itself.'

'That's impossible. I was a baby once, and *I* never screamed. I was precocious. Though I was a mere abbreviation of what I would become, I was already brittle, loathsome and fatuous.'

'A brittle baby?'

'That's a contraction for *brilliant* and *little*, of course.'

'But surely you couldn't have been a loathsome child,' said Ada, glancing up and down at the loathsome adult.

'Of course I was. *Loathsome* is a contraction for *loquacious* and *thoroughly toothsome.*'

'And *fatuous* is a contraction, then?'

'*Fat* and *fabulous*. I was simply adorable.'

'What does *adorable* mean?'

'Dull.' The Duchess fanned herself with a programme folded into pleats, not unlike the one the executioner had been devouring. 'You haven't seen my Cheshire Cat or my kitchen maid, have you? They're conspiring against me, no doubt. Sidling up to the prosecution and whispering all sorts of innuendo.'

'Off with her head!' roared the Queen of Hearts.

'My, the trial is proceeding at quite the clip today, or perhaps they've moved on to pudding,' said the Duchess. 'I daren't loiter or I'll be called as a witness, and the only thing to which I can reliably attest is that, as a witness, I am nothing if not unreliable.'

'Should I trust anything you say?'

'Not all babies are brittle, loathsome and fatuous. The ones who are deserve extra kisses. Remind me to kiss my own baby the next time he lifts his snout from the trough.' With this she gripped her skirts with hammy, washerwoman fingers. She set out across the lawns as if wolves were after her.

'I don't care to go before no judge,' said Siam. 'Mercy in short supply here and everywhere.'

'We must find Alice,' said Ada, 'or I must. Do you want to wait here for me?'

'There ain't no waiting,' he said sadly. 'You leave, you don't come back.'

He looked as if he knew what he meant better than Ada knew. She didn't want to pause. She didn't want to be unkind. But it seemed that in his life Siam had seen a sort of sadness that Alice had not. Alice was younger. Untried. Alice, Ada decided, needed her more. 'You can trust me,' she said to him, and reached out to his hand. But he pulled back as if she might burn him.

All of life hinges on what one does next, until finally one makes the wrong choice. But was this that moment? 'Alice, I'm coming.'

CHAPTER 44

Rhoda brought the tea. Lydia chose to sit at a distance. She pretended not to notice that her father indicated that she should pour. The governess took up the teapot with vigour.

'Was the visit with Mr Darwin what you would have hoped?' asked Miss Armstrong.

Mr Clowd slid his head peculiarly, describing with his chin a sort of S-curve that had fallen into italics. It resembled neither a nod nor a negative shaking. Or perhaps it was meant to be both at once. The governess continued. 'You are a brave man, Mr Clowd.'

'Bravery has nothing to do with times like this,' he replied. 'One gets on with it. Mr Darwin is circumspect in his remarks. But it's clear he can't reconcile the instability of the species — transmutation, or evolution, as it's now being called — with the faith of his fathers. I believe he can no longer conceive of a benign Godhead who could allow his daughter Annie such suffering. He tried with great delicacy not to go this far in his consoling words, but I'm not a fool.'

'If it is spiritual solace you seek, you might turn to Vicar Boyce.'

'He *is* a fool.'

Miss Armstrong tolerated this attack upon her beloved employer with alarming equanimity. Lydia sank in her chair, curving her spine in a way that would have elicited a correction from her mother.

Miss Armstrong stirred her tea. 'You must rely on your own instincts, Mr Clowd. As the American, Emerson, wrote in his First Series, "Character is centrality, the impossibility of being displaced or overset".'

'I did not imagine a governess might read Emerson's *Essays*.'

'She might do. But the essayist's point is about the urgency of not being dislodged from one's deepest beliefs. No matter how beset one might be.'

'Perhaps Emerson's comment is wrong. Perhaps we are meant and made to shift our beliefs. If it is a choice between being consistent or being wilfully blind . . .'

'If we are "made" or "meant", then someone must have made or meant us. But in any case, if you abandon the faith you shared with your dear departed wife, where does that leave her?'

'It leaves her wherever she is,' he admitted, looking at the carpet. 'Missing. Unaccounted for in heaven and no longer registered upon the earth.'

This was intolerable. Lydia said, 'I have no use for tea, after all. My mother died, Miss Armstrong. She is, consequently, dead. She had a big head like mine and Alice's and it's my opinion that it simply exploded.'

'For shame,' said Miss Armstrong, but mildly. It was not her place.

Lydia's father said, 'You aren't welcome, Lydia, if you're inclined to be discourteous. Go and locate Alice as you ought to have done earlier. And that boy, too. It's time they were home.' When Lydia didn't arise, Mr Clowd turned back to Miss Armstrong. 'Darwin found Siam charming. Darwin told us that one of his first friends at Edinburgh was a black man, a former slave, who taught him how to stuff and mount birds. I believe Darwin's deep aversion to slavery must date from this time. He had a falling-out with the master of the *Beagle* over a difference of opinion on the subject, as I've been told.'

'It seems inconceivable to me that there can be more than one opinion on the matter.'

'Mr Winter wouldn't have had to rescue that child if everyone agreed with you. Mr Winter's hope in visiting Mr Darwin was to solicit a testimony from the great man in support of Negro emancipation.'

'I don't know the American mind, but I should imagine that the remarks of the prophet of evolution would not be persuasive to those in the disassociated southern states.'

'Perhaps not. Still, as Americans go, he seems a kind young gentleman, that Mr Winter.'

'I wouldn't have had the chance to notice.'

What a liar you are, thought Lydia. The room fell silent as the adults sipped their tea. Mrs Brummidge or Rhoda must have gone to the garden well. The sound of the flywheel muttered into the windows like the whirrings of a mechanical insect out there in the slackening sunlight.

Mr Clowd observed, 'Darwin's professor, a certain Mr Sedgwick at Cambridge, wrote to him to say he feared that the popularization of his notions would serve to "brutalize humanity". I think those were the words.'

'We are quite brutal enough, I fear.' Miss Armstrong hefted up the tray of scones and proffered it to her host.

Mr Clowd shook his head as if to clear away evidence of the futility of human affairs. 'How is Ada coming along, then? I haven't laid eyes on her since the services.'

'Frankly, I don't hold that the iron corset and brace will succeed in correcting her posture, nor promote elegance of movement. Thus improving, eventually one must allow, her hopes for marriage and its subsequent rewards.' Miss Armstrong flushed a tempered pink at the mention of marital satisfactions. She sat a bit more upright upon her cushion, perhaps without being aware that it looked as if she were taking pride in the architecture of her own uncorrupted spine.

'She's an odd little clod, from what I've seen.'

'The arrival in the Vicar's household of a beloved infant boy has, I fear, delighted the Vicar and exhausted his inattentive wife to the point that correct governance of Ada has gone into arrears. I have spoken too freely, perhaps.'

'I thought it was your job to govern Ada.'

'Indeed it is.' Miss Armstrong settled her teacup. 'I have allowed myself to be delayed out of respect for your grief, Mr Clowd. No opportunity to acknowledge your loss had hitherto presented itself to me. I am indeed a governess. I shall be off at once. Perhaps we might walk together, Miss Lydia?' She stood. Mr Clowd stood. They both turned to Lydia Clowd.

'I'm not walking with a governess, I have no need of one, *myself,*' said Lydia with a doomy and suggestive intonation meant to wound, and wound it did. But Mr Clowd put his hand out to comfort Miss Armstrong's elbow. 'Oh, is there no end to the bonnyclabber of it all?' asked Lydia. Expecting no answer, she proceeded out the door of the parlour, leaving her father inappropriately alone with the governess of the Boyce household, and to Hell with them both.

CHAPTER 45

Without Siam, Ada hurried around a stand of creamy viburnum. The sound of the assembly grew faint. It became distant, screened off, the way the sound of the sea at Sandown was hushed when Miss Armstrong closed a window, complaining of the breeze. Ada felt as if a great glass box had descended from the sky to muffle the proceedings of the trial, if trial it were. Or the performance. Or, she thought, to muffle her.

A great glass box upon her! Ada noted that lately her thinking had gone colourful.

The viburnum formed a sort of closed grove. A wind turned itself over in the branches. The flowers lifted and settled in succession, as if they were whitecaps churning upon a shore. Poking out from them was a beached bathing machine, its steps descending to the grass. A figure in great black robes was sitting on the top step looking disagreeable. Ada knew at once who it must be, but she had no idea how Her Majesty might have got here. She was far too substantial to fall down any hole.

'We are lost,' said Queen Victoria. 'Wherever we meant to be, we are not there.'

'I beg your pardon, Your Majesty. Is there any way I might help?'

The Queen said, 'We doubt it very much indeed. Go away. Come back. Where is the Solent, do you suppose?'

'I'm not very good at maps, Your Majesty.'

'We find ourself in a garden amongst a set of lunatics and

one-offs. Amusing, and novel to be sure, but we are disturbed by the diversion from protocol. Have you a sweetie?'

Ada had nothing to offer the Queen. 'This is a garden party, not a bathing strand. Still, I believe you would find something to eat shortly if you came down.'

'We don't hunt for food like commoners. Food is brought us. Though perhaps we ought not to partake, for fear this is an underworld of some sort and we should be detained for seven years, or at least until springtime. We are like unto Persephone. We don't suppose – that is, it would be too much to hope for – you haven't by any chance seen the Prince Consort among this rabble?' To herself she mumbled, 'We should be very cross indeed to find the Prince Consort had condescended to join this motley host.'

Ada knew that Prince Albert was dead, and the widowed Queen was steeped in mourning. 'I have no reason to think that dead people are at large,' said the girl cautiously. 'That is to say, I haven't seen any. Unless you're dead yourself.'

'We never would. We have obligations. We carry on.' The Queen's rolled shoulders were like balls of yeasty bread that wanted punching down. Her intelligent eyes in their pouches regarded Ada warily. 'We imagine we are indulging in some regrettable dream, provoked perhaps by a suspicious element in last night's prawn bisque.'

'I don't believe this is a dream,' said Ada, 'but if it is, you'd hardly be in *my* dream. I don't even know you. Shall I try to go and find the Hatter? Perhaps he managed to cadge some cakes from the table after all, and he'd be willing to share.'

'We saw some mad creature go by arm in arm with a rangy hare. We would care for no confections discovered in those pockets. But what have you in *your* pinafore pockets?'

Ada was glad she had put the seaweed packet in her shoe. 'My pockets are empty,' she said truthfully.

The Queen sighed, and then brightened up. 'But did you see the Tweedle twins, Dum and Dee? Oh, they made us laugh. We *were* amused.'

'I haven't had the pleasure.' Ada didn't want to be rude, but the need to intercept Alice seemed to be more urgent with every moment that she dallied. 'Would you excuse me?'

Queen Victoria put one elbow on her knee and rested her set of chins in her fist. She looked every inch the potentate in her waxy black bathing skirts, a crown of diamonds and pearls pinned into her greying tresses so it wouldn't float away in the event of a surprise submersion. She was thoughtful and sad. 'I had no childhood,' she said to Ada. 'I was groomed to be Queen from the time I was five. No one read stories to me, only tracts of English history. I sometimes have the urge to go back and study childhood from inside it, so that I might be a better mother to the younger ones. Now the Prince of Wales has grown into a man, and I didn't know so much as a pat-a-cake rhyme to teach him. No one had taught it to me.'

'I could teach you that. It's a quick one, and very satisfying.' Ada climbed upon the lower wooden step and took hold of Her Majesty's hands, which were clammy and not quite as clean as she would have imagined. Ada said, 'Repeat after me.'

'Repeat after me,' said Queen Victoria obediently.

> *'Pat-a-cake, Pat-a-cake,*
> *Baker's Man;*
> *That I will Master*
> *As fast I can;*
> *Prick it and prick it*
> *And mark it with V—'*

(Ada edited as she went, in deference to the Crown of England.)

*'And there will be enough for Her Majesty the Queen, Supreme
Governor of the Church of England, Defender of the Faith, and
so on and so on, and me.'*

'You?' said the Queen. 'I wasn't imagining I would share. I
have become hungrier than ever.' She shook her head. Ada could
hear the wattles on her cheeks softly wuffing. 'Even in our
dreams, it seems, the Prince Consort is gone. What satisfaction
is left to us?' She stood up with determination and effort. 'We
shall retire into private life even in our dreams.'

'You have your nations to govern. And your children to raise.
And it's not too late to read the books you missed in childhood,'
said Ada.

'Have you anything to recommend?'

Ada considered *The History of the Fairchild Family.* Unrewarding
and macabre. What about those uplifting tales of child martyrs
that her father was always pressing upon her? Perhaps not for
a widow. 'You want something nonsensical,' said Ada. 'Keep
looking. It will come along.'

'We need something to return our stolen childhood to us,'
said Queen Victoria sadly. 'We do hope it is not too late for
that.'

'It's very late,' said the White Rabbit, appearing just then by
the wheels of the bathing carriage and looking at his watch.
'You've missed the marionettes entirely. They've all been executed
and are pausing for a refreshment before the second show. But
the trial is about to start, and I must be there, as I have important evidence.'

Ada did not know if he was addressing the Queen of England
or herself, but the Queen had disappeared into the cabin. The
sound of soft snores had begun to issue out on little clouds that
smelled like prawn bisque. 'Take me with you,' Ada said, and
grabbed his proffered paw.

CHAPTER 46

It did not seem as if they ran at all, but merely that the leafy viburnum parted. The white blooms fluttered away like moths. They stood at the back of a panelled hall. It must be the one that had turned into a forest and back again, as to the left of the judge's bench stood the pedestal of the overgrown glass-topped table. Ada craned to see if the key was still there. It was, farther away than ever. Whatever advantage *this* key promised – a key to all understandings or a key to the larder – it was still out of reach. The table was a living thing and its central post was a tree trunk, growing by inches like Jack's beanstalk. Soon the key would be out of sight in the clouds above her head, and Ada would never escape. 'I am required at the bench,' said the White Rabbit. 'If you need me, shout and scream and jump up and down. I may not deign to notice you, mind. You've become common.'

'According to Miss Armstrong, I'm ungovernable,' said Ada. 'But I won't shout and scream, thank you very much. I've learned not to follow advice.'

'Very sensible, too,' said the White Rabbit. 'I never would.' He looked her over with a twitch of his whiskers. 'I think I like Alice better than you.'

'I do, too,' she said, 'but I'm not on trial, am I?'

'Not yet,' he said. He bounded away.

Now, at last, over the shoulders of various animals and other creatures, Ada caught sight of Alice. She was standing before the bench in a very Alice-like way. Her elbows were neatly drawn in at her waist. Her hands were calmly cupped, one in the other. She seemed neither alarmed nor bored, just attentive. Ada wanted to wave and catch her friend's attention, but she didn't dare.

The judge was the King of Hearts. The Queen of Hearts was marching back and forth in front of the members of the jury, hitting each one on the head with a flamingo. The flamingo and its chosen victim both squawked upon impact. Perhaps Ada could sidle around the various raucous creatures and collect Alice quietly, when no one was looking? Then they might make their escape.

The only thing that stopped Ada was the presence of Siam back in the garden. If she stood just so, she could still see the door in the wall, which was now the *door not a door,* but ajar. The light inside the garden was glamorous and fresh. Siam was waiting, somewhere. If she could only position Siam within her sight, she might manage to apprehend both Siam and Alice at once. Though what they three might do when joined together against the world! – for all the education this day had afforded, she could not yet imagine.

'Call the first witness,' said the King of Hearts.

'First witness,' shrilled the White Rabbit.

The White Queen's head emerged from a pile of chattering oysters near Ada. 'Oh, my, you're alive,' said Ada gratefully. She reached over and helped the White Queen climb out of the *mêlée.*

'It's nearly time to get back to the Duchess's kitchen,' said the White Queen. 'I imagine the baby has turned into quite the little hog by now. It will need its hoofs trimmed. Babies want tending, you know. And there's supper to put on.'

'Would you like your cloak back?'

'You need it more than I do, dearie. Save it as a souvenir, if you get out of here alive.'

'Oh, I'll manage that,' said Ada. 'I do think using it as a lift in my heel has evened me up. I feel quite the new person.'

'So do I. I think I may be a Lady Clothilde, or perhaps a cockle vendor named Mopsy Maeve.' The White Queen shook Ada's hand with formality and feeling. 'I *never* give advice, but were I you, I should go through the ceiling.' She didn't lift her head but just pointed with one ivory finger. 'It's the only way out of this madhouse, you know. Coming, I'm coming,' she called to the White Rabbit when he'd begun to shriek for her. 'And I have testimony that is going to blow the lid off this affair, believe me.' She shook the last remaining oysters from the folds in her garments. She walked forwards, a little bit of unorthodox regency. Very sure of herself, and content because of it.

'Goodbye,' whispered Ada. She imagined, if she did manage to escape, that the ones she would miss were the White Queen and the White Knight. Generally adults were a failure, but these two managed failure well.

But should she find a way to take the Queen's advice, when advice around here was regularly unreliable? In any event, it seemed that the chances to escape were drawing in. She must find Siam and urge him to come with her.

She ducked through the door into the garden. The place was still and beautiful, but the only life it had was of the inanimate sort. No caterpillar upon the rose made nasty comment, no rose replied. The sunless shadows were deepening. The trees had grown extra boughs. Great drooping swaths of greenery, like theatre curtains, came folding in. Nothing could be heard from the courtroom behind her, though the door was still open; it had not yet swung closed. All was as still and silent as the world in the slowed growth in a photograph. Though the leaves swayed, they made no rustling.

'Siam,' she said, almost frightened to break the silence. 'It's time to go.'

He was there beside her. At first he looked at the ground. 'I ain't going,' he said in a mumbly voice.

'You can't stay here, Siam, because I can't stay. I have to get Alice back to her father. He would suffer so if she didn't return. He's had too much to bear already this year. You must come with me, or you'll be left here all alone. I mean, with them.'

'They cain't hurt me any strength. I been hurt enough elsewhere.' His chin poked up, his eyes were guarded and brave. 'Whatever mind I got, it made up.'

'You'll miss the world.'

'Little left to miss.'

'Your memories, though. Siam! They'll haunt you.'

'Thought of that. I don't want those memories. I going back to the Wood of No Names. I do make myself a hut in there, I know the how-to.'

Ada didn't feel she could do everything that needed to be done. Who was she, anyway, to say that he was wrong? But she had no time to argue. 'I must return to the courtroom, if it hasn't drifted away already. Siam. If you change your mind, come through the door.'

His expression was wry and unreadable. Maybe if she were an adult she might interpret it. She couldn't grow up on command though, finish the job while he stood there looking like – like that. It was getting late.

'I won't say goodbye, in the hopes you'll have a change of heart.'

'Change of mind, change of heart. What I need, change of skin.'

She threw her arms around him, wordlessly. She ducked away.

For once the transmuting world had not revised itself, at least in no way Ada could tell. She tiptoed behind a tea-trolley piled high with celery and boot-laces. She peered about. A pack of playing cards was assembling at the front of the room. At the bench, the King of Hearts was trying to win at noughts and crosses, using a salamander as a pen and a slice of bread as a paper. He poked the salamander's tail in a vaguely familiar pot of marmalade, but the salamander kept twisting about and licking the juicy compote off its tail before the King could make a mark on the bread. 'Very tricky game, this,' he was muttering to himself, 'but I'll master it yet.'

'I've so enjoyed myself, we must do it again sometime,' the White Queen was saying to the King of Hearts. 'I especially enjoyed the recitation and the Highland Fling. I never saw a Highland flung so far as that! Now, if you'll excuse me, I have one very tired little piggy at home who needs some mash slung his way. It's not his fault, you know. That he is such a little brute. Being birthed is hard work.'

'So is being dead,' replied the King of Hearts.

'Call the next witness,' whispered the Queen of Hearts to the White Rabbit.

'Alice!' cried the White Rabbit.

'If you please,' said Alice. 'I won't come. I have nothing to say today.'

'But you must,' said the King of Hearts, absentmindedly sucking the tip of the salamander's tail. 'Otherwise we're all at sixteens and sevens.'

'That's sixes and sevens, I do believe,' Alice corrected him.

'No, we left the sixes in the larder, and we brought the sixteens by mistake. Nothing adds up. Do you see what I am up against? Now come here and take your place like a good girl, and do as you're told.'

'I'll come,' said Alice, 'but I can't promise to be useful.'

'Little girls often lie,' said the King of Hearts helpfully. 'You may be useful despite yourself.'

Ada found herself thinking, Alice, don't fuss; just go there and do their bidding. No one can pay attention for more than a few moments in this place.

'Do as he says, or your head will spin,' roared the Queen of Hearts.

'Stuff and nonsense,' said Alice with what, to Ada, seemed uncharacteristic insolence. But who knew what sort of a day *she* had had?

The Queen of Hearts turned crimson. 'Hold your tongue!'

'I won't,' said Alice.

'Off with her head!' shouted the Queen.

'Who cares for you?' asked Alice. 'You're nothing but a pack of cards.'

An upheaval, a commotion, a seism shuddered the room. The standing army brought several suits against Alice. Ada watched Alice raise her arm to her eyes to fend them off. She fell backwards against a marble statue of a dodo. She slumped against it, limp, rag-like. Her eyes were closed and didn't open.

'Call the next witness!' said the White Rabbit to himself, and did so. 'The Jabberwock!'

CHAPTER 47

Miss Armstrong reclaimed her gloves from the table in the passage. It was time to put folly behind her. She had taken a false step somewhere early in the day, and she would pay for it for the rest of her life. She only hoped it would not come to pass that someone had seen her pursuing Ada, catching up with her, and tumbling the girl into deep water. If Miss Armstrong had done that – had acted on her dreadful fantasy – she could not recall it, and that much was true. The amnesia of the hysteric. She would say so to the magistrate, or the warden of the gaol at Oxford Castle. For now, there was nothing left awaiting her in the benighted Vicarage but the accusations and recriminations of a hard-lived day. Another one. She left the Croft by the front door, unable to imagine she might return, and soon.

Lydia wandered out, too, through the kitchen garden. Darwin had been right; there would be no downpour. The afternoon was pulsing with the last energy of daylight, which had turned dry and flecked. It was the time of year when English evening can take three hours being absorbed into night-time. But dusk was out there, ferrying in from the Low Countries, halting and hovering off the coast of Essex, picking up strength from dark waters, gathering its moods and forces.

For the first time Lydia began to wonder, seriously, if she should be frightened for Alice. It would be a novel exercise, both because Lydia's capacity for raw emotion had been so overwhelmed in recent months that, until today, she'd imagined she could never feel anything deeply ever again; and also because, well. Alice.

Alice was immortal. Alice was immortal in a way their mother had not been. It had to do with Alice's strange gravitas, her unerring solidity. Death wouldn't come near her. It wouldn't dare. And mind, this was not the immortality that children demonstrate, blindly, children who, because they do not know they will die, behave as if it cannot happen. Sooner or later we grow into deserving our own deaths, somehow.

Alice was different. She was rectitude and curiosity and bravery; she was stubbornness and tolerance. Something of her childhood always seemed to slip out of her — as if through permeable membranes — as if she were one of Darwin's anomalous specimens. Alice was an ordinary child whose unordinary childhood seemed an infectious condition to those who came near. Lydia often felt like a bit player, a common sort of business, her own existence merely some adumbration ornamenting the life of her weird sister. The spider under the table at the Last Supper, the cat who looked at a King. The King is history; where the cat went next is not recorded.

And yet — Lydia had been pacing along the path as she mused, and now she had reached the place on the riverbank where she had stopped earlier that day. Look, she'd dropped her book of commentary on Shakespeare's midsummer dream, and she'd never noticed: there it still lay in the meadow-grass — and yet, and yet. Who else to play the part of a bit player in the life of a child? What is a parent but a sort of valet to the royalty of innocent youth? With Mrs Clowd gone, and Mr Clowd lost in grief, Alice had no one else. And Lydia was all she had, and not enough.

Lydia paused and sat down, and leaned against the tree. She put her hands to her face. She didn't care to think about her mother. She wasn't ready. Unwelcome, indeed forbidden, a memory rose up through the flooring of the day, a memory of Jane Clowd. Lydia tried to resist it but memories are anarchic.

Some winter morning. A few years ago. Jane Clowd had come back from London. A visit to a surgery in Harley Street. Alighting from the carriage onto the glossy, ice-slicked cobbles of the lane. Leaning to thank the driver and turning to greet her girls. Her hair had fallen out of its pins on one side. The bonnet was askew. Forsaking their December wear, the girls had pummelled down the path from the Croft, meaning to throw themselves in her arms. Against the cold, one hand was still immersed in a white muff of rabbit fur. The other hand, gloveless, was reaching towards her girls.

CHAPTER 48

Ada began to lunge towards Alice, to make sure she was not badly hurt, but a sound behind her made her turn. Every-one else was swivelling and pulling back at the same time. The playing cards built themselves into a kind of pyramid. The Queen of Hearts flew to the top, claiming the advantage. The Tin Ballerina and the Tin Bear tossed their kites into the air, and climbed the ascending strings like circus roustabouts. The Cheshire Cat allowed his tail to appear, flicking viciously and offering no doubt as to its owner's disapproval. The White Queen was gone, having retired into domestic service. The Duchess was trying to hide behind a fan made of a splayed hand of Clubs, a royal flush, who were objecting though to no avail. Having hopped upon the bench of the King of Hearts, the White Rabbit circled madly, crying, 'Beware the Jabberwock, my son!' No one in the room, as far as Ada could tell, had a son or was a father. All told, this seemed a rather parentless set of circumstances. So she couldn't imagine whom he might be addressing.

Indeed, the only person not contorting or shrieking in alarm was Alice, because she was insensate against the plinth of the marble dodo.

'I do hope you don't mind,' said Ada to the White Knight, who had risen creakily to his feet. 'I would like to climb upon your shoulders.'

'Fancy serving the likes of you. Mind your bony knees, sir. But be my guest.'

She scrabbled up and peered over the heads of various hedgehogs, lollygagging sarsen stones, gossiping potatoes, a walrus, and some roses that looked vaguely familiar but turned snootily away. The back of the room, as if unable to shake off a habit of recidivism, had returned to forest. The wall was junglefied, hung with vines, lurid with unseemly fruits and lascivious flowers. Shrieking gibbons and toucans conversed in an unfamiliar patois. The floor of the forest remained tiled in black and white squares, but those tiles were being tossed forwards like flotsam on a storm-hurried tidal surge. Soil from beneath the floor spat up. The Jabberwock was approaching from below.

'An underworld beneath this one?' said Ada to the White Knight. 'Has it no shame?'

He answered, 'Did you seriously believe you would ever understand all that there is to be known?'

Then a roar shook the room. It was like the collapse of a textile mill into a dry riverbed. The King of Hearts replied, 'Silence!' in the most timid, mouse-like voice he could manage. 'If you please.' The Jabberwock, sandy dirt streaming from its iron jaws, clawed its way up from some unimaginable tomb.

'Oh, you,' said Ada. 'I might have known.'

'You are on speaking terms with this monstrous threat?' cried the Queen of Hearts.

'In a manner of speaking. I mean, in a manner of non-speaking.'

The Jabberwock finished dragging its clawed grips from below. It stood flexing its skeletal wings. There was rather little head, so one had to be impressed that it could manage to roar at all. The circlet of neck brace, which buckled in front, seemed to serve as the mouth, for as it contorted in slits and ovals, an assortment of enraged industrial sounds was heard. The rib cage had grown iron extensions. They unfolded into pinions, like the skeleton of a bird. Where its knuckled, prehensile feet had come from, Ada could not imagine. They looked something like bundles of fish forks.

'*You've* had yourself quite the adventure, I see,' said Ada.

The Jabberwock developed a couple of grommets on its upper brow and blinked them at her. She wondered if it would recognize her now it had grown so grand.

'I'm afraid the excursion is over,' she told it. 'It's time we returned.'

'If you mean to take your little pet home, now would be the proper moment,' said the King of Hearts, quaveringly.

'Off with its head,' added the Queen of Hearts, though without conviction, as it really didn't have much of a head.

The Jabberwock flexed its wings and circled above the crowd in the courtroom, snatching at a sleeping dormouse. It deposited the dormouse into its open maw, but the dormouse simply dropped through and landed into a barrister's starched wig, snoring all the while. Ada thought, Is that all that happens by walking into the mouth of doom?

'For a creature with a magnificent wingspan, it doesn't seem to be able to attain any useful altitude,' said the King of Hearts, diving flat upon the judge's bench to avoid being taken for a ride.

'Naturally,' said the Tin Ballerina. 'Its wings are merely an armature. The air goes right through them, providing no lift. It needs skin, it needs an area of resistance. Like the cloth of a kite.'

'I have just the thing,' said Ada. She took off her shoe and removed the seaweed cloak. It was none the worse for compression. As Ada began to unfold the triangle of material, she said, 'Come here and behave; it's time for you to knuckle down and accept correction. It's for your own good, mark my words. You'll never be much, but you can be better than you are now.' The sentiment wasn't hers but Miss Armstrong's, retailed of a morning after shucking Ada of her nightgown and submitting her to a brisk scrub. Hateful words, but they came in use now. The Jabberwock settled docilely enough upon the head of Humpty Dumpty, who held still and kept his eyes squeezed shut, pleading that the iron claws did not clench, or the yolk would be on him.

'I'm fried,' he whimpered. 'This is it. I'm finally cracking up. All the King's horses and all the King's men won't be able to put me back together again.'

'Shhh,' said Ada. 'Don't worry. Why the King's horses and men? I'm sure the Queen's attendants are much more capable when it comes to managing eggs, but no one ever mentions *them*.' She nimbled upon the helmet of the White Knight and flung wide the unfolded cloak.

'This will only take a moment,' she said to the Jabberwock. 'There. That's much better, don't you agree?'

The Jabberwock turned its head this way and that to regard its wings, newly fledged with seaweed. It fitted perfectly, as if it were custom cut by a Parisian seamstress. Oysters in a crate began to shriek in joy and beg to be taken for a ride.

'We've no time for that now,' she told the oysters. 'Come now, Jabberwock; we must be off.'

'Must you leave so soon?' asked the White Rabbit. 'Can't you leave sooner?'

'It'll be as if I was never here at all,' promised Ada. She stood still. The Jabberwock came forward and settled itself around her. Ada buckled the strap about her neck and another about her waist. She fitted her arms into the rings that clamped tight in her armpits. The Jabberwock had grown, but so had she, it seemed. The fit was even keener than it had been this morning. Of course, Ada was accustomed to being squeezed into the apparatus below her clothing, and now it was overlaid, and public, like a suit of armour, but she had no intention of stripping to her smalls in a court of law, however deranged the audience.

When she was properly corrected, she said to the White Rabbit, 'You're the time-keeper here. What time is it?'

He looked at his pocket-watch. 'It's very late indeed.'

'Then there is no time like the present to say goodbye.' With this Ada flexed her new wings and pushed her way to the front of the room. Humpty Dumpty exhaled sulphurously. Ada knelt below the bust of the marble dodo. 'Alice, my dear, it's time to go home.'

Her friend was breathing nicely enough. She didn't stir. She was lost in some dream-world. With the strength allowed by iron reinforcement, Ada reached down and collected Alice beneath her armpits. She hugged her close, as if she were a tender mother, or even an older sister, and Alice a child who had fallen asleep under the dining room table.

Rising, Ada cast a glance towards the door to the garden, but the door was closed now, Siam behind it, and the sign that had said

KEEP OUT.

now said

KEEP IN.

and there was no longer a keyhole.

Those who are roped into bed at night often fall into delusions of flight. Though usually a dreamer of commonplace notions, once in a while Ada had enjoyed dreams of flying. So she was hardly surprised to find herself not only capable but skilled at this exercise. The wings of her iron cage flexed mightily. She moved upwards in a spiral, leaving behind without regret all those creatures, their idiocies and affections. She disobeyed earlier advice and looked up rather than down. She could see in the underside of the glass tabletop a reflection of the impossible wonderland, a looking-glass simulacrum that could entice without either endangering or offering reward. On the other side, above the glass, which had widened to roof all of this underworld, rested the key. If she could leave with the key she could, perhaps, come back someday and rescue Siam. When he was ready to allow it.

As she was pumping her iron wings to batter against the glass ceiling and claim the key once and for all, a hoary old tench drifted above this world. He waggled his brown fins at her. He swallowed up the key, tag and all. He swam away.

She felt a sudden rage. The ascent of the human creature — one has to fight to be born, after all. She bashed against the glass with every ounce of her might. She would break through, she would. So she did, being a child with more force of intention that she'd previously allowed herself to acknowledge. The tabletop split with a jagged line. The glass shattered. An ocean of water rolled over Ada and Alice. Whatever was below the wave was lost to view. Anything that might be above it could not be imagined. There is a limit to the nonsense even a dream can attempt.

CHAPTER 49

Gasping for air, Ada pulled Alice safely into the shallows. The bank was low. Though Alice was limp and heavy, Ada felt in herself the strength that accompanies terror. She saw Lydia still sitting by the tree, though the light had shifted across horizons, and the air had lost its morning warmth. Lydia had nodded off over a boring text. Good. The tracks of a few tears showed on her cheek. Ada was able to hoist Alice the several feet to the trunk of the tree. Alice murmured something that Ada couldn't quite make out, but Alice's voice even in nonsense syllables sounded like herself. Ada believed she would be all right.

She turned to look in the river to see if she could find that damnable tench. If he was in there, taunting her, she would come back another day with a fishing pole and a handful of bait stolen from the larder. She'd go to work to rescue Siam. There was always a key somewhere. One only needed to know where to start looking.

For a moment the river seemed to cease its endless motion. Perhaps Ada was having a dizzy spell of some sort. She leaned over the surface, which was as still as a waxed tabletop. She caught sight of her bemused face. Her hair was drenched and bedraggled. She had lost the perfect form of the ringlets that Miss Armstrong always tortured into her hair. But a fierce light rain was beginning to fall (no matter what Darwin had predicted). Ada would seem only to have got caught in a downpour.

She glanced back. Alice was already beginning to stir. She had crawled nearer and placed her head in her sister's lap, and murmured her sister's name. In her own somnolence, Lydia had let her hand fall over Alice's outrageous brow, comforting.

Ada looked back at her reflection again, to see if she could find on her face any trace of what she had been through, the details of which were beginning to fade. She could not. All she could see, drifting in the water now like the wreck of a dressmaker's dummy, were the struts and buckles of her closest companion, drowned for good. If it had once worn a seaweed skin, all that was dissolved away.

She left it there. She straightened up – straighter than she'd ever managed before – and wondered which way in this fantastic world to turn.

A girl, even a clumsy one, who had managed to rescue her best friend might prove qualified to serve as a big sister.

A white rabbit hopped out from a stand of grass. It was that hour when rabbits feed, though they don't often come out in the damp. It twitched at something appealing, but then turned to look at Ada. It had no waistcoat or pocket-watch. Still, it stood upright, as if a lone member of some honour guard. Then, without possible doubt, the rabbit pointed at the path towards Alice's home.

So Ada gave a curtsey, the first real curtsey she'd ever managed in her life, and set off at a startling clip to surprise Mr Clowd and Mrs Brummidge, and whomever else might be lingering at the Croft of a summer evening, and to apologize for having lost a gift of marmalade, somehow, along the way.

CHAPTER 50

Darwin had nodded off at the rocking of the train. When he woke up, he guessed they were nearing Paddington. London was purple in the midsummer gloaming, so its lamplights, just being lit, made a fever rash of amber sparks. He glanced at Josiah Winter, the only other traveller in the carriage. The American was distraught, picking at his nails. Darwin knew about fretfulness as well as he knew about anything else. To distract the poor fellow from whatever he was suffering, Darwin made a remark. The noise of the train wheels muffled it.

'I beg your pardon? Did you refer to a catastrophe?' asked Mr Winter. 'Or epiphany? – I misheard.'

'I was musing on the notion of a cataphany.'

'I don't understand.'

'Cataphany. My own word, from the Greek *cata,* meaning down, and *phantazein,* to make visible. Also the root of *fantasy,* don't you know. Cataphany: an insight, a revelation of underness. The findings of Odysseus in Hades, interviewing the shade of Achilles. Or Gilgamesh, hunting Enkidu. Or even, meaning no disrespect, the Christ arising after three days in Hell. What sort of revelation can occur in perfect dark? What would Eurydice tell us if Orpheus had been able to bring her back?'

Winter gave a shrug, looked away. A sequence of lights and darks played across his shuttered face. He shuffled a few ha'pence in one hand. A sound like small jangling keys, or the links of a slack chain falling upon one another.

The elderly man continued, out of mercy and out of curiosity, for that was what he was like. 'Let me put it more scientifically. If separate species develop skills that help them survive, and if those attributes are favoured which best benefit the individual and its native population, to what possible end might we suppose has arisen, Mr Winter, that particular capacity of the human being known as the imagination?'

– finis –